From the mind of

TESHELLE COMBS

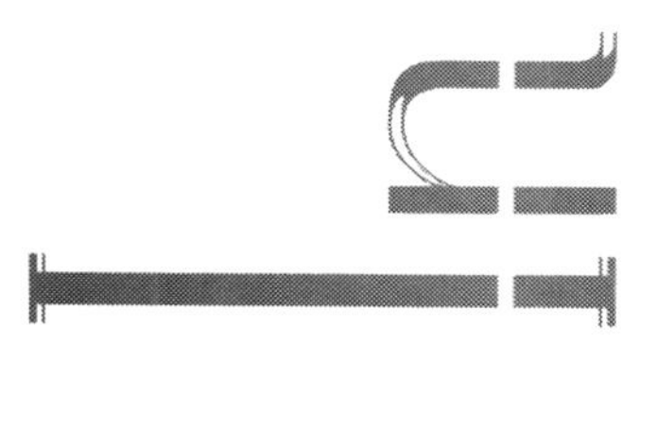

The worst love story ever told.

Teshelle Combs Books

Manufactured in the United States of America.
Book layout and design by Nate Combs Media.
Hardcover ISBN: 979-8370736766
Paperback ISBN: 979-8369869994

This story is currently available in serial format on the Kindle Vella platform.

When the raging is over, I will still be holding your hand.

Ep I

Good Boy

No.

I imagined saying this to the med who told me to hold my arm out and try to stay very still. But I did not say it to her, no matter how alluring my fantasy. It was not a speaking day for me.

She tightened the rubber strap around my upper arm, tapped her needle, and sunk it into the flesh of my inner elbow. I did not wince. Good boy. Then, she squeezed the anti-illness into my veins.

I noticed the problem before she did. I'd spent enough time analyzing my own skin to know something was wrong. Her injection was not precise enough. Perhaps she had forgotten to double check that the needle point matched my pore size. I had smaller pores than most. Lucky me.

Behind her white mask, the color drained from her face. Her eyes began to dart, looking for a way to fix what she had done. But I knew better. She had made an error. It would be found but not forgiven. She blotted my arm with a cotton ball and placed a small bandage over the incision site. She motioned for me to leave.

I stood up and made it one step before he came in.

"How are you looking, Marrow?" he asked me.

He knew I could not answer. My jaw was wired shut. It would remain this way until the surgery completely healed. I had another few days. So the cycle went.

He glanced at the med, assessing her sweating brow and sallowed disposition.

"Show me," he said.

I lifted my left arm to him. He peeled the bandage off, careful not to damage my flawlessness any further. There, floating in the amber pool of my complexion, was the tiniest mar. A pin's prick.

He straightened up, his dark eyes growing harder than they already were.

"Do you understand, Marrow, how valuable you are?"

I could not answer.

"Do you understand what this costs us all? This flaw?"

I tried not to look at the med, but my eyes flitted over to her anyway. "Do not worry about her," he said. "We all know she will pay for what she has done."

What had this stranger done? Inflicted a blemish on the skin of a Glimpse. The skin that was to remain perfect in every way for all of time. She had sealed her own fate when she tampered with mine. I wanted to reach out, to touch her cheek, to tell her I was not angry. I was not worried. I was not ruined.

But I could not touch her. I could not tell her. I was to be touched. I was to be told.

"Report for your removal," he said to the med, without even looking at her.

As she stood, setting her equipment down for the last time, tears slipped from her eyes. I wanted to reach for those tears, to rub them between my fingers. What did they feel like? What did she feel like? Such things interested me, but I was not to have such interests.

She left, her head hung, half her face still behind her mask.

"You must not worry," he said to me. "Not about the med nor the flaw nor anything at all. Worry creates creases, wrinkles, lines, discoloration. Do you want those things, Marrow? Do you want to be a prisoner to age and repulsion? A Glimpse of death rather than life itself?"

I could not answer. And if I could have, it would not have mattered.

A Glimpse is meant to be seen, not to see. To be enjoyed, not to enjoy.

The med would report for removal. Her body would be devalued, then dismembered, then, if she was worth anything, harvested and repurposed. But I did not pity her. How could I? She had been allowed to live. She would be allowed to die.

And me?

I could not answer.

Ep 2

He Always Does

For those of us who were on a walking day, it was time to practice.

Seven of us present. We clustered up, most to share the latest gossip. I, of course, would be listening. Not that I ever shared. It was not one of my traits to be gossipy. But I did enjoy listening. It was an art in itself.

Iris was already going full speed. I wondered whether she ever stopped talking. Perhaps she even got a special allowance for extra speaking days. *Her jaws must be so strong.*

"Can you believe what they said about Dewy?" She smiled and tossed her head back, showing the very backs of her sharp, white teeth. It made her purple hair cascade over her shoulders. "They completely screwed up her leg day. And now"—she paused for dramatic effect—"she has a limp."

A few of the other Glimpses gasped in horror, but most were just excited that something was happening at all, even if it was to someone else and not them.

"That is a horrible thing to happen so close to testing," Whimsy said, her voice as airy as her name. Her eyes looked dreamy with her beaded lashes. It was difficult to detect any true concern in her cloudy gaze. "What if she is not healed in time?"

Iris waved her hand. "Hafiz will make sure she is perfectly well. He always does."

As if she'd summoned him, Hafiz entered the room, which was as plain as he was. Every inch was covered in mirrors except for the floor. The man—our teacher, mentor, guardian—stood in the center of the room and clapped his hands, which made my ears ring.

He wore a long, cream coat, and underneath was a suit of clothing that fit so tight it looked like skin. His necklace was glistening rows of diamonds from his collarbone to his waist.

"Altogether now," he said. "Morning stretches."

We formed a line and began. Bending, bending. Tearing, tearing. If Hafiz walked by one of us, he reached his brown hands out and stretched us even further until our bones creaked and our tendons groaned. But we did not complain.

"And now, one at a time."

This was my least favorite part, though Glimpses like Iris enjoyed the solo attention. She glided to the front without hesitation, and we all watched as Hafiz critiqued her form.

"For you, heavier steps, Iris," he said. "Place each step. You will be seen. You will be noticed."

She adjusted again and again, her eyes focused, droplets of sweat running down her temples.

Next was Cleft. Named for his most distinguishing feature, he was a bit of a collector's item. He would never be universally beautiful, but someone enamored by the character of his face would pay enormously to see him. When he walked, he led with his chin, just a bit, so it was prominent but not exaggerated.

"You are bouncing," Hafiz said. "Is this a game to you? Are you a pony to be ridden."

"No, Hafiz. I will not bounce." And so Cleft went a few extra times around the room until I noticed his ankles were trembling.

"Come, Marrow."

I was always startled to hear my name, even though I knew he would call it eventually. The dread in my stomach congealed into a hard knot of panic. But I could not—could never—let it show on my features.

I stepped forward, keeping in my mind what I had been taught since before I could remember any teachings. You Are Marrow. You go deep, deep down. A mystery. Too vital to be bought or sold. The source of life itself.

And so I walked like Marrow, with my body hardly moving, yet taking up much space. With my head lowered but my eyes lifted, as if I knew a secret. Maybe all the secrets.

"Well done, Marrow." Hafiz waved me back to my spot in line.

I felt the regard of the other Glimpses turn to me, burning with contempt. I was not the favorite, no. Hafiz did not have favorites. I was simply the best. And I paid for it every day.

Ep 3

It Takes Skill To Quiver

"I heard you had a med killed today."

Cleft, Stardust, and Iris. I knew without opening my eyes who it would be.

I stayed very still on my cot, observing. I did not want to fight and certainly could not argue. Either of those would get us punished. They were not worth it. I hoped they quickly got their fill and decided I was not worth it either.

"Let us see the great wound that cost her her life." Stardust, his lilac hair loose around his shoulders, leaned closer so that his tresses tickled my nose. "Show us, beautiful Marrow." He tilted his head over me. "Unless you'd rather tell me?"

He reached out and traced a long, perfect finger across my jawline, sending a rush of pain through my face. I did not flinch because flinching was not a thing we were permitted to do.

"You can pretend to be perfect, but I can see the pain in your eyes, Marrow. You are not invincible like you think."

"Get out," someone said from the doorway to my sleeping area. "Now. Or I will tell Hafiz you hurt him, and he will give you extra walking practice tomorrow."

I almost didn't place the gentle voice. She spoke up so rarely.

The three tormentors left, and Blush approached my cot. Her soft pink, almost white hair rose and fell in ringlets around her ivory face.

She stood over me until I sat up. I did not think she had ever actually spoken to me before. No one knew what went on in her mind. She was not taught to share it, like Iris and Stardust were. She was a fleeting glance of a Glimpse. Better felt than heard or seen. Her presence was a notion.

"Testing. That's when we will see which one of us captures the eyes of the Grands."

She stretched out a quivering hand. Really, it took great skill to quiver on demand like that. She rested it on my cheek, and it was the softest thing I had ever felt, barely causing any pain at all. We were not supposed to touch one another, or really anything. It could cause blemishes, bruises. Those like Cleft, Stardust, and Iris broke the rules. It was in their desired nature. But Blush and I were not that sort. Still, her fingers were the softest things I had ever felt. Softer than any gloved hand or sharpened needle.

Without changing an ounce of expression, she curled her fingers and squeezed so that the pressure in my jaw exploded, my incisions reopening inside my mouth. I tasted the blood but could not cry out and did not think it worth it to touch her. She would report me then. And I would be adjusted.

So I waited, in agony, until she was finished torturing me. She did not smile or otherwise show pleasure when she was finished. Only fluttered out of my sleeping area. There was no door to close behind her.

I swallowed the blood inside my mouth, hoping doing so would save me from having to show Hafiz, from reporting who had done it, from watching the gentle Blush being adjusted.

I lay back down in my cot trying to capture a few moments of rest before I was put in front of the mirrors again. I did not want to see myself. I did not want to know myself. I did not want to be myself.

If I could have done something to get myself removed—like the med who marred me—I would have done it. But there was nothing. I was destined, fated to repeat days like this. Over and Over. If I made a mistake, I was adjusted, not removed. Adjusted until I was flawless. Beautiful. A Glimpse of perfection.

Tuck Me In

So I closed my eyes and imagined a world where I was at least invisible. And I cursed God Across that I was not born mercifully plain.

Ep 4

Bare Minimum

"Bellanueva Anamaria Morales De Leon. 7,345.11 days old. Born Here, not There."

I tapped my fingers on the desk so fast they probably blurred. *Come on, come on, come on*. The line had been so long, I was pretty sure people were doing it on purpose. But finally, at last, it was my turn to receive the terrible service we all deserved.

The bookwatcher clickedy-clicked on her computation device as if she had never seen one before. She squinted at each of the letters on an individual basis like a new one might have popped up and surprised her if she weren't careful enough. Finally, she wheezed, "I'm sorry, clever girl, but I don't see your name in here."

Oh my god, you have to be kidding me. "Did you type it in correctly?"

The woman slid her glasses down her wide, freckled nose, almost scraping off one of her enormous moles, so she could eye me. "I know how to do my job. Don't get smart with me."

"Getting smart is all I'm trying to do, miss," I said. I swooped my wavy, curly, sob story up into a messy bun on top of my head. Easier to think without it in my face. "Bellanueva. Like one word."

"Oh," she said. "One word. Okay."

I looked down at my watch. *I am cursed. Actually, legitimately cursed.* While I waited for no reason, I started tracing back my family line, trying to determine which De Leon had sabotaged a sacred burial ground or something of the sort. *I bet it was Tatarabuelo. That bastard. That's why my life is like this.*

"Ah, here we are. Bella...new...ava. Ana...mo...ria...."

"Oh please, please just scan me in. Please. I'm going to be late."

She smacked her lips. "You know, If you scheduled your days more efficiently—"

"I swear to you, mi vida, if you scan me in right now, I will come back after this test and listen to as long a lecture as you've got. I will even take notes at your feet. But please. Let me in."

She glared at me and then held up her scanner. I lifted my hand to it, but she pulled away at the last second.

"Fifty gol. For the rush. And the attitude."

I slammed my hands on the desk and pressed my forehead to the aluminum. I jerked back up and wiped at my face. *Gack. Why is everything Here so sticky?* "Do I look like I have fifty gol, lady?" I gestured to myself: baggy brown pants that used to belong to my brother, a tank top I was certainly outgrowing even though I was skin and bones, and a watch with a cracked face that only worked when I was already late.

The bookwatcher shrugged and went back to her comp. I sighed. *God obviously hates me. So what do I have to lose?* And then I jumped, belly first, onto the counter, like a baby seal stuck on an iceberg. I swiped the back of my hand under her stupid scanner, and took off sprinting down the corridor.

I smashed through the door of the testing center, eliciting gasps from everyone already properly seated, awaiting instructions.

"Hi, hi, hola, konnich', guten." I looked around the room, hands on my hips, trying to catch my breath. "No, uh, no seats left huh?"

The instructor stared with the blank eyes of a serial killer.

"No worries. Be right back. Hang tight."

I darted out of the room and across the hall, flinging open another door. *Empty seats. Yes.* "Don't mind me," I said to those assembling for their test. I tried to lift a chair, but it weighed a thousand units. "Really solid investment, these chairs. Wow. You guys really care about sitting." I proceeded to drag it across the linoleum floor and out into the open space of the corridor. I imagined it wasn't squealing like a lobster in boiling water the whole time. But it was.

I held the door to my room open with my foot and hoisted the chair inside. Finally, I collapsed into it and gave the instructor a thumbs up. "Nailed it."

He would have sighed if he weren't obviously some kind of robot. "Pencils out."

Pencil. Oh no. I shoved my hands into my pockets, sure I had brought it with me. I had, but when I pulled it out, it was in pieces. Probably from careening over the desk to scan myself in.

No matter. There was still a point to one of the stubby little pieces. I could do anything given the bare minimum. Literally anything. I had to. There were no other options.

The instructor set paper in front of each of us. "Eyes to yourself. And begin."

My usual pep talk. Short and to the point. *If you want to live and not die, you get every question right.* I had no idea what everyone else used for self-motivation, but the stark, unfiltered truth usually worked for me.

Ep 5

The Soggiest Letter

"...and you don't hear that?"

Ah. A familiar sensation brought me back to the room. *Someone's unhappy with me.*

My second oldest sister was yelling, the strap of her dress off her shoulder and the hem out of place from hoisting a discombobulated toddler onto her hip.

"Bel? Are you even listening to me?"

I was not. But I decided to try really hard to fix that since Confía seemed more sweaty and flustered than usual. "Say it again," I offered.

She spoke louder and slower, like being hard of hearing was my problem. "How long has he been crying like this? Didn't you hear him?"

I looked around the room at the five or six children, all wailing or whimpering in some way. "Which one?"

She stomped away with a huff.

I shrugged, "Confía, they are all always crying. You ask how I didn't hear? I ask how you can still notice these things."

"Because I pay attention, Bel. Because someone has to pay attention."

I followed her as she shuffled around the kitchen, balancing the chunky, gooey toddler, Kechick. He was still bawling, a string of snot dangling out of his nose and pooling onto her dress.

"Okay, I'm sorry. I'm sorry. I wasn't being helpful. I zoned out. But...I can help. What do you need?"

"You can hold him for once," she said.

"Blech." I took a step back with a grimace. "What... *else* do you need help with?"

"Dios, Bellanueva." She rolled her eyes and kept sorting through the kitchen drawers.

"What are you looking for?"

"The...the thing. That you roll things with," she said, her head inside the cabinet.

"Oh the rolly thingy! I think dad took that."

She straightened back up, suddenly even more stern. "Took? What do you mean 'took'?"

"Uhhh...he took it. For something. Outside?"

"Oh?" I could tell Confía was angry when her eyes got wide but her voice got calm. "Is he making bread out in the garage? Baking a cake in the yard? Because the rolly thingy is for *food*, Bel."

"I mean...maybe?" *Ha. Yeah right*. He was probably using it to unclog a pipe or prop up the chicken coup.

"Well, I need the rolly thingy. Tell me you can handle that."

I looked around at the screaming children, most of whom needed their diaper situations addressed. Our other siblings were no doubt havocking about the streets. Soon, disgruntled neighbors would come to complain about which climbed a tree they weren't meant to and which spray painted a cat. When I weighed all that, going to find the rolly thingy was not so bad a gig.

"Okay, I will find it, but then I need to study."

The biggest eye roll from Confía when I mentioned studying. "Go, go, go."

I took my time on the cement staircase, letting the rough steps settle against the soles of my bare feet. But before I made it to the back of the yard where my dad was tinkering, no doubt destroying Confía's cooking device, a truck pulled up.

The mail.

My stomach dropped. I hated being the one to receive the mail. It was the worst. Nothing but bills and late payments and citations to appear in judgment rooms. And whoever had to hand the stack to my father became the "one who handed the bills" to him. The whole day was basically unfit for the discard heap after that.

I flipped through the haul and froze when I saw my name in big, square letters on the top. A couple letters were spelled wrong, but sometimes I wasn't even sure if I knew how to get my own name right. Regardless, I never got mail. Not ever.

I stuck the rest of the letters between my knees and ripped my envelope open. The letter inside. My test. I didn't think I'd get it back so soon. I scanned the letter, looking for the numbers, for the score. Anything lower than one thousand would keep me in Grit. I would do pretty much anything to get out.

When I was 2,400 days old, my father told me the only way I would ever get out of Grit was if I did it myself. No one would help me. No one. And to do it, I would have to be literally perfect.

There. The number. The score. I braced my heart, my stomach tightening and threatening to void itself. *Please, please be higher than one thousand. Please.*

6,000.00.

I flipped the letter over to see if maybe it was a scam. A mean trick. No. Official seal of the Grade was on it. 6,000 was a perfect score. An absolutely perfect score. There was no way. No way I could have pulled that off. But in my brain was that little tingly feeling that said, *Heck yes. Yes. I knew it. I knew the whole time.*

"Mail?" my father asked.

I jumped, dropping all the other now meaningless letters and such that I'd held between my knees onto the ground.

He sighed, wiping filthy hands on his stained pants. "I hope none of those were important."

I stuffed my test results under my armpit. "Hey, um...have you seen Confía's rolly thingy?"

My father, his belly poking out over his pants and his shirt stained with motor oil, squinched his nose. "Seen what?"

"The rolly thingy. You know...for rolling."

"Oh. That. I used it to prop the engine door open. Over there."

I looked over his shoulder at the thingy, which was covered in grease and grime and very surely holding up the hood of a vehicle.

"Fantastic."

He sorted through the mail with a scowl and a couple curses. "The Grand is coming Here."

"Yay?"

"No. No yay. They'll make us fix everything up for them."

I scratched my head. "Oh yeah. I hate clean stuff."

He eyed me with a scowl. "Who do you think has to pay gol to meet these standards of theirs?"

He shoved the letters at me hard enough for me to stumble backward, threw his hat on the ground, and returned to his engine.

I tried not to forget that my perfect score was still under my arm, but already, I could feel it slipping.

Ep 6

If I Call Your Name

Lights that could blind a person. But I could not squint, even though they burned my dark eyes. They wanted to see my eyes, the stark dilation of my pupils. The mirrored floor was cold against my bare feet. The room was chilled. They wanted to see the tiny bumps that pricked my amber skin when I shivered.

"Let us see your hair," they said. I bent my head, and a gloved Grade ran his hand through my black hair. The straight, silken locks were kept just at my shoulder blades. The Grade explored my texture, the state of my ends and my scalp.

I had every inch of my naked body explored, from the beds of my nails to the rotation of my ankles. I walked, moved, stretched, and froze as they commanded, until my body was drenched in sweat, the cold of the room a distant memory.

"That's enough," the Grade finally said, his face hidden behind a suit of white and large, thick goggles. "You may join the others and await your results."

In the holding room, I joined the rest. The last of twenty Glimpses to be tested. I sat down and tried not to be nervous. But it was impossible. My mind kept drifting to what would happen to me if I failed this particular test. Usually, it would be adjustments, surgeries, unbelievable pain, and humiliation.

But this was a benchmark test. Those who passed would be presented to the Grands for the first time and would be eligible for specialized study by the Grades. A life of refinement. Of being seen and not touched.

But fail this test, and we would be sent to Here, not There. We would live among Grits and lower level Grades. We would be at risk to be touched, handled, harmed. And since we were Glimpses, we would live forever this way.

If we passed, we would be beauty for those who desired it. If we failed, we would be beauty for those who disdained it.

Hafiz stood in the center of the room with a few Grades. He wore glittering gold and shimmering eye shadow. He looked regal. Magnificent. The Grades were all dressed like white-clothed monsters to me. No faces or adornments. Just...calculations.

"If I call your name," Hafiz said to the room of us Glimpses, you will travel to Here, and your new journey as a Glimpse will begin. If I do not call your name, you will remain There, and your journey as a Glimpse will continue. Do not think of this as a punishment or reward. It is only natural. And what is, will be."

He took one last look at all of us. That's when I realized it was the last time I would see some of these Glimpses again. No matter if I went to Here or There, we would be separated forever.

"Collar. Dewy. Wonder."

As he began calling names of those who failed the test, the Grades stepped forward to guide them out of the room. Only not all of them rose and departed with honor. Dewy gripped her chair and locked her knees, her pale skin growing whiter. Wonder screamed with the kind of terror that only came at night during desperate dreams. Collar stood and tried to run. I could not guess where he thought he was going. There was no way out of being a Glimpse.

The Grades were not equipped for manual labor. They struggled to wrestle the failed Glimpses into submission. And Hafiz made the mistake of continuing with the list. He called seven more names at once. Some shrieked from their seats. Others tried to fight.

Stardust fell to my feet where I sat and wrapped his arms around my knees. He gripped my legs with his fingers. "Please," he said, looking into my eyes.

"Marrow, please. Help me. Don't let them take me. Don't let them do this to me."

A Grade took hold of his ankles and began dragging him away. But Glimpses were strong. Our bodies well-conditioned. Our nutrition perfect. Stardust kicked his legs and dug his nails into my skin.

"Please," he screamed, his gray-blue eyes leaking tears we were not allowed to cry. "Please, please. I'm beautiful. I'm beautiful."

I put my hands on his. It was all I could do. I did not try to stop him from scraping at my legs or weeping or wailing. But I felt his skin. One more time. Even though all he had ever done was try to hurt me, to destroy me. It was the only way I could connect to this Glimpse I had known my whole life, who I would never see again.

Finally, they got him off of me and took him out of the room. I could hear them all howling and sobbing as they were taken away.

Ten of us remained in the holding area. Some wept silently. Some shivered and held themselves. Others, like me, did not move at all.

"Iris, Whimsy, Cacophony, Cleft, Muse, Gradience, Whisper, Helix, Lavish...and Marrow. Congratulations. You will remain. Glimpses of what can be." Hafiz beamed, though he was flustered, his scarves askew and his eye shadow smudged from the chaos.

"Now," he continued, "the real work begins."

Ep 7

From Here To There

The only way I managed to report to the Here Center on time was to sneak out of the house before dawn showed its crack. Pretty difficult to do since Confía was up with the youngest of our siblings so early.

I tried to look decent for such an important day, but it wasn't really possible. My clothes were hand-me-downs of hand-me-downs. No amount of scrubbing or loathful shaming would make them look new again.

Cyrilus. That's who the letter said to meet. So I waited for him in the lobby of the Center, trying not to step where the motto was plastered on the floor. "Here Is Where We Shall Stay." I always felt like I would be cursed if my feet touched the lettering, doomed to live my life in squalor and mundanity.

"If you can hear the sound of my voice, it means you are the brightest of the bright this dim corner of existence the world has to offer. You will be transported to There, only for a few hours. You will observe Grands, face to face, and take note of their customs, their needs and desires, their ways and mannerisms. You will then be tested again, after which more definitive placements may be given to you. The brightest will become Grades. The dimmest will return to Grit, living your days with great effort and little reward."

The speaker was a wiry man with a gray and balding head and a good number of liver spots. He wore thick glasses and leaned on a cane. But he spoke like he was the one who invented words.

There were over a dozen of us. All young, of course. They stopped testing only 100 days older than me. Confía had already failed any chance at being a Grade. She would be a Grit forever. And no one could ever become a Grand. They just...already were.

Jostled around by the rough Here streets, I sat quiet in the large, poorly maintained bus. All the way in the back. Most others with me remained silent as well. But a few wanted to know what scores the others had received.

"I knew for sure I would receive over the 1,000 mark," one of the boys said, wearing what I'd call a sneer if I were being nice about it. He said his name was Horatio and asked for people to call him Ratio, because he 'thought it was clever.' "But I was floored to find a 4,200 on my letter."

A couple others gasped. That was a high score, they muttered. They asked Ratio for some pointers.

"Keep a keen eye on the competition," he said, his piggy nose held high. "You don't have to be smart. Just smarter than them."

"That makes literally no sense," the girl next to me whispered.

I shrugged. "No? I thought it was brilliant. Don't be smart, just be really smart. I think they should paint that onto the ground over at the Here Center. To inspire the dumb ones."

She snorted. "You're funny."

I grinned. "Comes with the brain, I'm afraid. Package deal."

She offered her hand. "I'm Mango."

"I am sorry. I have no filter, and I thought I heard something ridiculous just come out of your mouth. Did you say...Mango? Like the fruit?"

She enacted a frown. "No, idiot. Mango like the person."

I chuckled. "You can call me Bel." I pretended to toss my hair over my shoulder. "I think it's quite clever."

Mango sighed. "Okay, fine. Yes."

"Yes?"

"Yes, I'll be your friend. You don't have to beg."

"Sweet." I sat back on the torn leather of the bus seat. "I never was good at acquiring friends."

"What score did you get, Bel?" Mango reached into her pocket and offered some of the raisins she had stashed in there.

I wasn't about to start being picky. The last thing I'd eaten was dry noodles out of the pack. Pocket raisins were a feast food. "Thanks for these," I said, mid-chew, deflecting the question about my score.

"Wow. That means you either did really well or not that great." Mango was no dummy. She picked up on my dodge with no problem.

I shrugged. "What about you? What did you get?"

She winked. "You know...I actually hate raisins."

We settled in, and I watched the landscape change as we went from Here to There. I'd never been so far from home. Never seen anything but potholed roads and sagging roofs. Children with no shoes and even less parental affection rolling dice in the streets. But on the way, I could see everything change. The sun shone through green hills. The trees grew with big ancient trunks. The roads went from gravel to easy, luscious pavement.

The landscape broke into what I would describe as a divine city. The buildings were all chrome and white, glistening under billowing clouds. Water rushed from fountains as tall as the heavens, cascading into pools that seemed to stretch for infinity. People glowed as they strolled on pristine paths in between the many buildings.

We got off the bus and I wanted to hide. Impossible. Impossible to feel so...lesser than. Like someone had been hoarding me in their garage for 7,000 days before depositing me There. I tugged at my baggy used-to-be-white shirt, wishing I could make the tiny holes along the frayed hem disappear.

"We are severely underdressed," Mango whispered as we stood on the street awaiting instructions.

A few people from There glanced or even stared. We did not fit. That much was certain.

Come on now, Bel, I told myself. *Did you come here to feel insecure about your appearance or did you come here to be a Grade? No one wants you to be beautiful. They want you to be brilliant.*

So I straightened my sloping shoulders and started observing.

The people all had perfect posture. I made a note. They walked erect, sort of gliding over the ground rather than taking clunky steps or shifting their gait.

Here, where I was from, men walked with widened stances and broad shoulders, their hands in fists to show dominance and power. To prove they were worthy of wives and children. So no one would try to take what they had.

And the women walked with slinking hips and firm steps. To show they were capable of both labor and childbearing and to lure in admiring husbands who would risk their lives to protect them.

But There, I noticed not just men and women, but everything in between. And everyone walked as if they had nothing to prove. They were already proven. *So they are aware not only that they are superior, but that their superiority cannot be threatened.*

I made a calculation. Grands did not like to be reminded that others were beneath them. That was boring. Maybe even icky. Rather, Grands would prefer to be shown that something exists above them. *I bet they value inspiration.* The construct of their city alone was evidence that I was correct.

"Come," said Cyrilus to our group. "You will sit and eat with Grands. And then you will see the Grand Tower. After that, back to Here and on to testing."

I couldn't explain why. But I had always known that if I could just see the Grand Tower, I could make sense of it all. Something I'd learned about in the books I'd stolen from the Reading Center but couldn't fully grasp without experiencing it. Like a missing puzzle piece.

And finally, with a score like mine and wits for days, I had earned the chance to see it.

Ep 8

What One Berry Can Do

"You will stand here and observe. Do not interfere. Do not take. Just look and listen. Thinking is also highly encouraged."

The food smelled so good it hurt. I literally had to keep my hand pressed to my belly. The raisins Mango gave me had long since disintegrated in my overeager stomach acid. I was running on empty. We all were.

You know when someone is really, truly, deeply hungry by how quiet they get when food is present. And our entire group was steeped in silence. I felt hollow, suddenly, as the plates of meats and berries and breads were passed around.

I tried to focus on other things. On the spectacle that was the lofty hall. The ceilings were twice as high as those in our Here buildings. They domed and loped, the architecture curving and arching to create the illusion of endless white space. The windows let in so much light that it made me put my hand over my eyes to keep from squinting. *Is the sun itself brighter There?*

I made a mental note: *the Grands like to see and hear everything in great detail, whereas Grits will use clutter and noise to smother our many flaws. We ignore, they illuminate.*

I observed a man I would describe as too tall. His legs sort of buckled when he walked, yet he glided just as gracefully as all the other Grands. His hair was so long, the tips of it swept the floor. He was not worried about it getting dirty, I was sure. There was no dust There.

Cleanliness is not a task There; it is an assumption.

The man had a strange way of eating. Soon, I noticed all the Grands ate in this disturbing way. Rather than placing a strawberry into his mouth, the man stuck out his tongue, placed the strawberry on it, and curled the sides of his tongue toward the middle. Then he suctioned the food into his mouth with a slurp.

Gak. Okay, the eating is strange, but why?

Once the food was in his mouth, he closed his eyes and chewed slowly, his body swaying back and forth slightly, his mouth in the slightest shape of a smile. The best word I could think was that he looked 'pleased.'

Pleasure. I almost shouted it out loud. *He savors the pleasure of eating. Here, we chomp and chomp because the point of eating is to reverse hunger as quickly as possible. But There, they eat to enjoy it.*

We seek satiety; they seek pleasure. I corrected myself. *They seek nuanced pleasure.* I had a feeling novelty was highly desired among the Grands. Again, I reminded myself: *they're bored.*

I wanted to hear one of them talk. Speech could say a lot about people. But we were standing too far away from the Grands to pick up on anything.

I tiptoed to the back of our group, then slowly inched my way toward one of the tables laden with food. It was hard not to snatch a berry or two, but I was not about to get disqualified from my entire future because of snackage. Still, it was a risk. If Cyrilus saw me close to the food, he could assume I was stealing even if I wasn't. *Yet, knowledge like this could put me just enough ahead of the others.*

A couple Grands floated near the table. I listened as best I could.

"Dazzling. Heartfelt. Wondrous."

"Confirmed and reciprocated. Delightful. But still dreary, yes?"

"Oh yes, yes. Still dreary. And cumbersome."

"And."

Whaaaat? I did not expect that. Not at all. I would have killed to have paper and pencil with me. But my memory would have to do. *They speak...in descriptions?* I heard not one subject or object in their syntax. No verbs or action words. I almost squealed with excitement. *What a discovery! Could there be anything more interesting? Or as a Grand might say, "Interesting, yes?"*

I was about to make my way back to our group when the tiniest Grand stepped in between the group and me. He looked like the faeries I'd seen in books when I was a child. Almost translucent skin, tiny bones like a bird's, and a sharp nose. His eyes were blacker than black.

"Strange," he said. His voice warbled, as if he were hitting multiple musical notes.

I didn't think I was allowed to talk to Grands, being a Grit and all, so I just stood there with my arms flapping at my sides.

"Lost?"

I cleared my throat. "Uh...no. I'm with that group over there." I pointed to the others.

The bird Grand stared. It took me a moment to realize he didn't understand what I said. "No," he repeated back to me, choosing the only words I'd said that were comprehensible. "That. There."

I tried again. "I—" *No. No subjects.* I tried again again. "Lost? No. Together." I pointed to the group.

The bird Grand twisted to see them. "Oh. Dingy. Smelly. Sad. Sad. Sad."

Wow. Even less of a filter than me. I gestured to the hall. "Dazzling," I said. "Beautiful."

He cooed. "Dazzling, yes. Beautiful, no. Yet dazzling."

I decided to push my luck. I pointed at the bird Grand himself. "Subtle," I said, trying to warble my voice like his. "Subtle and...epic."

Boy, did the bird Grand like that one. He sort of trembled and put his hands to his cheeks. The white and lavender hairs on his head stood up like he'd been shocked. "Epic, yes? Epic!"

He reached to the table, plucked a golden berry with the longest fingernails I had ever witnessed—times a thousand—and held the fruit out to my mouth. Reluctantly, I leaned forward and took the treat from his hands, trying to balance it on my tongue as I'd noticed other Grands doing. Couldn't get my tongue to obey me. Not exactly graceful.

He fluttered off, walking up to other Grands, putting his hands on his cheeks over and over and crying, "Epic! Epic, yes! Epic!"

By then, my entire group noticed I was not observing goings-on at a safe and approved distance. I stared back at them, half a berry sticking out of my mouth like I was a suckling pig on a Happyday. I chewed it quickly in case Cyrilus told me to spit it out or something. It was the sweetest, most succulent thing I had ever ingested.

"Oh my god, wow. Wow." I licked the juice off my chin with my tongue. Not a drop could be missed.

"Not the best with instructions, are you?" Cyrilus asked, his frown so deep he could have lost the bus keys in there.

"The...uh...the bird Grand wanted a compliment. I thought it would be rude to ignore him."

Cyrilus squinted at me. "It would have been unforgivable. But how did you know he wanted a compliment, Grit?"

I shrugged, still high off the berry. "No one dresses like that unless they want a compliment."

Cyrilus tried to look all regal and dogmatic, but his lips twitched. He turned back to the others and said nothing more about my breaking the rules.

Que afortunado. I made two friends in one day. And if Cock-a-doodle Dandy counts, that's three.

Horatio, the arrogant fool from the bus, snuck up behind me. I figured that out because he put his hot wet breath on the back of my neck.

"Mi amor," he said with the worst accent I had ever heard. And then, I kid you not, he kissed my nape. Just a little peck. Enough to make me vomit in my mouth. I could feel the sweetness of the berry fading from my palate. But he wasn't done. "Take my spot, and I'll kill your whole familia."

When I whipped around to cuss him out, he had already crossed to the other side of our group.

Three friends. And one enemy.

Ep 9

Can't You Feel It?

"What the fleas and festers was *that*?" Mango asked as we shuffled back into the bus. "Why were the Grands so...weird?" She shivered, rubbing her brown arms.

"It was un poco upsetting," I said. "But so interesting, don't you think?"

"No." She shook her head, small locks flinging around her plum-shaped face. "Not interesting. I'd go with...nightmarish."

I kept my attention on the streets as we drove along, soaking up as much information as possible. "We're only getting started, Mango. Can't you feel it?"

Mango blinked. "Feel what?" She pulled her feet up onto the seat. "Is it a spider? Oh no, is it a rat?"

"No, no, relax. Not vermin." I pushed her legs so they flopped back down. "I mean...don't you feel *fate*? It's moving us."

"Say what now?"

"My abuela taught me. Fate. It means things are moving in a certain direction, and we get caught up in the flow. Sometimes it brings us to ruin. Sometimes to glory. But we can't help where we go, so might as well make it a fiesta."

Mango grinned. "Your grandma sounds badass."

I nodded. "She was."

Mango frowned. "Dead, huh?"

I nodded. "Yes. I suppose that was her fate."

"Was she just like...super old?"

"No." I pretended no images flashed in my brain. I pretended I felt nothing. "They shot her."

Mango's eyes widened. "An old lady? Why?"

"Long story."

Luckily, Mango knew well enough to let me be. I needed to focus. We both did. The information we gathered on this trip would help us pass our next round of tests.

We piled out of the bus at Grand Tower, and I forced my brain to take it all in at once. The tallest structure I had ever seen. It stretched to the sky in a spiraling point. Not simply white, but iridescent, with subtle blues, pinks, and golds. Magnificent marble stairs. Looming pillars many times larger than any one person. The windows glistened with refracted light, making my eyes water.

"The windows themselves are made of carved diamond," Cyrilus explained.

"Diamond? How do they see anything through them?" Horatio asked.

They don't. Whatever was inside was so worth gazing upon, a view of the outside would have been wasted.

We jostled up the stairs and through enormous archways. There were rows and rows of balconies curving around a spectacular room. It seemed as if something belonged in the center of the room. *Why are all the balconies surrounding an empty space? When the Tower is filled with Grands, what are they looking at? Why come to the Tower if there's nothing to see?*

I had hoped the Tower would hold some sort of meaning. *Why? Why do the Grits live Here and the Grands There? Why do the Grades observe and calculate and measure? Why are we all alive, doing what we do when we do?*

"If you've all had your fill of the grandeur, we will return to Here, and you will begin your next round of testing."

Cyrilus led the group back the way we came. And I followed a few steps behind, searching for any last-minute clues to my questions. Finally, devoid of hope or hints, I sighed, throwing my head back in despair.

That's when I found it. I craned my neck as far as I could until finally, I resigned to lying on my back on the pristine floor.

The Grands don't stand on the balconies and look down. They look up.

In the center of the domed ceiling, almost too high up for me to see clearly with my naked eyes, was a clock. As if it floated among the clouds. With precision and to my shock, it did not count around, like other clocks. Its numbers went down. I closed one eye and traced the numbers with my index finger, making the shape of a crescent moon. The other side of the circular face was blank.

The clock...counted *down*. Top to bottom. From one million to zero.

Its golden clock hand hovered over the number 214.

I realized my group had left me, so I sprang up and raced outside and into the bus. I was not easily spooked in life. Not by the murderous gangs of the Grit nor the unsettling glitz of the Grands. But my stomach twisted inside me when I pictured the distant celestial clock. I couldn't say I knew the reason, but I regretted seeing it. I wished I had never gone to the Grand Tower.

I wished I had never looked up.

Why are we Here? Why There? And what happens when that clock runs out of numbers?

Ep 10

For Keeps

Hafiz flipped through the papers that held details from the latest big test.

"Very good, very good," he said to himself. Then he paused. "Hmm...it seems the Grand standard for finger length has changed. We will have to adjust."

I did not feel dread at that news. Not yet. If it was a decrease in length, it would not be so painful. But if it was an increase...my stomach twisted in on itself at the thought.

I did not show this contemplation on my face. Hafiz would have lectured me if he knew I entertained worry of any kind. I wanted to stand up and walk about; running helped me calm my thoughts. But I was reclined in a cushioned chair, shirtless, a long tube running from a machine to my belly.

Some Glimpses rumored that Grands ate with their mouths. That there was food that came in many colors and shapes. That the Grands smashed the food with their teeth and swallowed. It went down their throats and into their bellies. And that this made them very happy.

I had never eaten. It was not good for my teeth, and I could choke when I swallowed the mashed food. It was also more difficult for the body to absorb the anti-illness and beauty-builders it needed at the pace they were needed. A tube in my abdomen made it all so much simpler. Glimpses were to appear complex but remain very simple. Always.

Hafiz finished reviewing my test and set the papers aside. "You really have done so well, Marrow," he said. "There are many Grands already very interested in you. They have not seen your likeness, of course. But there are whispers of your beauty all over There." He held up his fingers but he was not holding anything for me to look at. It was only for emphasis on his words. I did not understand why people did that. "Marrow, you must understand what you display. Yours is a deep beauty. Almost primal. Like the planet itself carved you in its womb. You will remind the Grands not only of what they could be, but of what they once were."

"But I am not a Grand," I said. "And Grands are not Glimpses."

Hafiz scowled. "You must use your imagination, Marrow."

I thought about that. "Could you be more precise about what I am to imagine?"

"The nuances of your beauty." He had that tone of voice. Terse and pitched high. He was frustrated with me.

But I did not understand. And if I did not understand, how could I perform this beauty for the Grands? "You want me to imagine nuances?"

Hafiz scoffed and walked away. To a med he said, "Schedule a finger extension for this afternoon. Then, he will meet with analysis."

A finger extension. I was not sure if it was a necessity or if Hafiz was punishing me for my ignorance. He should have expected my ignorance. I was taught almost nothing. We pieced together the world from bits of gossip and eavesdropping on meds when they thought we were not listening.

The med looked a bit sorry when he removed my feeding tube and prepped my hands for the procedure.

"Will I be put to sleep?" I asked. I hoped the answer would be 'yes'. But if Hafiz was angry, he might not have ordered a sleep injection.

The med's white mask blocked his mouth. It made it hard for me to tell what he was feeling. I could tell by the eyes, though, that he was unhappy. Perhaps guilty. "You must report for analysis once the procedure is over. That would not be possible if you were sedated now." He wanted to apologize, but that was not allowed. Glimpses were not supposed to feel pity. Especially not for themselves.

The med placed a bite guard in my mouth to keep me from clenching my jaw too tight. He strapped my arms, legs, and torso to the chair with silk ties.

"Please try to keep from wrinkling or bruising," he warned. "Keep your face calm and your body limp."

He checked the dimensions for adjustments on his work order and began marking my skin. Black lines so he could see where to cut.

Go far away, I told myself. *Far away. And imagine your nuances*. For the next while, I was not in the chair with my hands being opened, my bones pulled apart and padded, my skin reassembled and adhesed. I was in the warm womb of the planet. And she was growing me there. She did not need to adjust me when I was with her. She thought I was beautiful. She made me for keeps.

Ep 11

Just Answer The Question

I sat down for the test, my dark hair piled on top of my head to minimize distractions. My chair squeaked beneath me every time I shifted. That was unfortunate. But I had a pencil this time. I was pretty proud of myself for that. *Prepared. Like a real Grade.*

Cyrilus handed out a strange little contraption. I'd never used one in a test before. Never seen anything like it. It was small, square, black. It had wires and little patches connected to it.

"You will place the electrodes on your neck and temples," he instructed, showing us how the little pads could be made sticky before being stuck to us.

This is weird. But everything about Grades was weird when all I knew was the Grit world.

"Now turn the device on using this button. And place it on the table in front of you."

I did so, and it crackled to life.

"If, at any point, you are unwilling to complete this assessment as instructed, you are welcome to leave the test, and thus the program, to continue your life as Grit. But if you choose to stay, you must adhere to the rules without question. You must also, of course, receive a high enough score on the assessment itself." He cleared his throat and then smirked, which made me nervous. "This device will monitor your hesitation. When you are unsure of an answer, it will detect finite, invisible cues that betray your own doubts. And it will administer a slight corrective measure."

A slight...what now?

"Remove or attempt to touch this device in any way, and your test is over. Verbal complaint. Over. Standing, shifting in your chair. Over. A question to me, the instructor. Over. Simply finish the test without distraction or hesitation. That is your best chance at passing. Merit and more to you. Begin."

The first question:

What did you notice about the lighting There?

Option A) Nothing in particular

Option B) It is beautiful

Option C) It is not harsh

Option D) it is illuminating

What kind of question is this? Nothing about mathematics or correct grammar use—*oh my GOD!*

The device's electrodes zapped my face and neck, sending a strong electrical pulse through my body.

Oh no, oh no, okay. Just answer the question.

I chose C. The Grands cared more about how beautiful they looked than how beautiful the light seemed.

I moved on to the next question:

> Why are the staircases There designed the way they are?

What? The staircases? I wasn't paying attention—oh my GOD, no! It shocked me again. That time was much worse than the first. Immediately, sweat raced to my forehead. *Just answer, Bel. Stop trying to think. There is no time.*

> Option A) The steps are beautiful and ornate
> Option B) The staircase material prevents slipping
> Option C) There were no steps
> Option D) The steps are placed close together

Option D. Not because I remembered what the staircases looked like, but because I remembered the Grands had tiny little baby bird feet. Like little mini horses or something. They probably couldn't handle gigantic, majestic staircases with those feet.

I moved on to the next question, but a few of the group cried out in pain. I could hear the buzz of their devices. When I looked up to see if they were alright, the device zapped me so hard that I almost cried out as well.

Do not look up, Bel. Pay attention.

I started another question, trying to ignore the person in front of me who was electrocuted severely enough for their whole body to stiffen and shudder in their seat. When the shock was over, they slumped, and their head lolled backward. With brief horror, I wondered if they were dead.

But then I decided that thinking about whether they were dead would ensure that I would be dead too. So I kept answering, my hands too sweaty to grip the pencil well, and my heart beating out of my chest.

I lost myself in the questions and answers, and the sound of screaming and the thrashing of bodies ravaged by electrical current faded away.

I kept one thought.

If you don't pass, you'll die, Bel. You'll die. You'll die. You'll die.

Ep 12

Words On A Page

"Where have you been all day?" Confía was washing the dishes, her hands moving so fast that suds flew out of the metal basin with each swirl of the rag. "I needed you, Bellanueva."

I bumped her hip with mine, nudging her out of the way. "I can do this. You go." I didn't mention the test or the trip to There. She had no idea I was even being considered for moving out of Grit life.

Confía glanced at the moon outside our small, square kitchen window, gauging the time. "He'll be back soon."

"I know. I'll finish these, Fi. You go."

She stood back, taking in the messy kitchen. Plates and pots piled on the tiny counters. Food splatters on the chipped cabinets. The tiled floor cracked and caked in mud from the dozens of footsteps that tracked in and out of the house that day.

"It's too much for just you," she said, her voice betraying how tired she really was. She was still beautiful to me, though. Her round shoulders, her curvy shape, her full lips and heavy eyelashes.

"I know how to clean, Fi. You worry too much."

"He'll expect it all to be done when he walks in here."

"He'll be drunk when he walks in here. And it won't matter what I did or didn't get done."

Confía leaned against the cabinet, her head in her hands. "Don't say that, Bel."

I sighed. "Okay. I won't say that." I gestured toward the big bedroom with a flop of my head. "They all asleep?"

She nodded, chewing on her fingernail. Stalling. "You didn't answer. Where have you been all day?"

"I had some stuff to get done."

She stood up straighter, immediately alarmed, her dimpled cheeks flushed. "What kind of stuff, Bel?"

"No, no. Nothing bad. Just school stuff. No big deal."

"You look pretty tired from this 'no-big-deal' school stuff."

"That's just my default expression. And look who's talking? You think you walk around like una princesa with little birds who braid your hair and bring you coffee?"

She smiled at that, though it was mingled with sorrow. Of all of us, Confía would have made a great princess. Then she sighed. Her face got that pale, a withdrawn look to it.

"I'd better go," she said.

And right on cue, my chest tightened, and I thought I might crack the dish I was scrubbing if my grip tightened any more.

"Fi, you don't have to do this." We had this conversation almost every night. Over and over. We both knew it by heart. It was my least favorite song.

"Bel, don't. How many times—"

"Exactly. How many times?"

"Until I don't have to anymore, Bel. So you don't ever have to."

I scoffed. "There is nothing you can do that will stop them from forcing me, Confía, and you know that. A hundred more days. That's the only thing they're waiting for. A hundred more days until I'm grown. This idea that you are protecting me, that you are sacrificing yourself for me...it's a delusion. It's not real."

"And what do you think I should do, B? Huh? Tell them no? Say, 'Sorry, Lăobăn, but my baby sister says I don't have to anymore'?"

"We could run."

She laughed. A spiteful, bitter laugh. "That is not possible for us. There is nowhere but Here."

"It worked for mom."

Now she'll either slap me or storm off and cry. We were pretty well rehearsed. And that was Confía's reaction any time I brought up our mother. But this time, she didn't get angry.

"*That* is a delusion, Bellanueva." She kissed my cheek. "And what I have to do—for you, for us—is because *she* was deluded. Deluded and selfish." She straightened her shoulders and jabbed a thumb at her chest. "This. This is real."

And then my sister left. To change her clothes and spray some cheap fragrance. To try her best to forget who she was for one night. And the men would line up. And pay their money. And take what they came for. All we would get out of it was another day where we were allowed to live. To struggle. To dread the night that was to come.

I tried to wash the dishes even faster. But Confía was right. It was too much for one person. Her bedroom was about to be occupied. And I could not be near it. I could not hear it.

So I left the dishes and the mess. I resigned myself to the fact that my father would rage when he realized I had not done them. And instead, I grabbed a stolen book and slipped out the front door. I sat on the curb, under the streetlights, and slumped behind an abandoned vehicle. Hidden enough to keep the night wanderers from noticing me. Close enough to hear if Confía screamed for my help.

Checking the cover of the book before I began was a waste of time. A courtesy to the author, really. I didn't care what I read anymore. Anything. Any words. Any subject. Any language. Even if I couldn't understand it. I read because the shapes of the words were exquisite. Because somewhere, someone wrote them down with the hope that another human would find them. That someone would understand something about the one who wrote it.

The first man showed up to our house for Confía, and I tried not to look away from my book to see if he was someone I knew—a neighbor or an old friend, an uncle or a cousin.

For a few hours, I didn't think about tests or Grands or what would happen to me if I couldn't get out of Here. I didn't think about my sister and strange men or whether the 'sleeping' children could hear what they were doing. I thought about nothing. I became words on a page. And I let someone else write my story for a while.

Ep 13

Mistakes

I kept my hands very still through the hours of questions. Any movements sent searing pain from my fingers to the rest of my body. But the worst part was the constant discomfort. It never left, filling my mind and causing distractions. Still, I tried to do a decent job, to be present, to be honest.

The interviewers were...boring. That did not help to keep my attention. Each with their white lab coats and matching face masks. I could not see their hair or even much of their skin. They asked the same sorts of questions. Over and over.

"What is your name? How old are you? Weight? Height?" These things were all in the charts Hafiz sent with me. That, or they were unanswerable. Either way, the Grades were wasting their time.

They measured me, requiring me to move my hands, which made my body seize, even if I did not wish it to. They squeezed my muscles and pinched my skin, trying to find why my beauty ratings were so high. Trying to replicate me.

After the tenth Grade was finished with me, Hafiz came to see how I was doing. He wore a net bejeweled with the tiniest pearls over his face. He adorned his eyes with thick, black mascara, so it was easier to see them through the white veil.

"What do you think of their questions, Marrow?"

What do I think? That was not a usual question for someone like me. "I suppose I do not think anything of them," I said. That was an answer Marrow would give.

Hafiz nodded. "Probably better that way. Let your mind go elsewhere. No need to worry about their incapabilities. The Grades are becoming quite useless. They have not pleased the Grands with their metrics in quite some time." He smiled through the veil. Bright red lips. "Besides. There is nothing they could do to improve your beauty, Marrow. Study as they might. They cannot even understand it, much less replicate or enhance it."

I sensed he was proud of this, as if he were somehow the one who made me so beautiful. But Hafiz was not a Glimpse. He only sculpted us.

Hafiz scoffed. "The next to take your measurements is not even a Grade. A mere fledgling. That is how desperate these Grades have become. Do not let her make a marring mistake on you, Marrow. Be careful."

He left, but there was no way I could follow his directions. I could only say 'yes' to whatever the Grades asked. If this fledgling wanted to mar me, she would do so. Other people had choices; I only dealt with consequences.

The one who walked in next was only given a white lab coat when she arrived. She took it awkwardly, as if she had never seen one before and did not know what to do with it. She shrugged it onto her shoulders but did not fasten its buttons. I could still see what she wore underneath. A loose, black shirt with a tattered hem and a worn image on the front. Her pants were short, made of rough materials, with holes and tears scattered throughout. Her shoes were scuffed and sullied. I had never seen anyone with this manner of apparel. And so I could not help but stare.

I noticed that she had an injury on her left knee. The skin was scraped and swollen, red and opened.

"You are injured," I said, concerned and unable to look away from her knee.

"Oh?" She lifted her leg so she could examine the site herself. "It's just a scrape. No big deal. It'll heal."

But I could not look away. I had only seen surgical wounds. They had clean, straight lines. They were bandaged and monitored. This person walked around with her injury untreated. Who was caring for it? Who was caring for her?

"Hey," she said. She waved her hand in front of my eyes to get my attention. I looked up at her. She smiled. "Ever been streetboarding?"

She had a different kind of smile. Her lips were not quite even. One corner of her mouth lifted higher than the other. Because of this, she had a deep dimple in only one cheek. I tried to focus on her question, but it was not easy. "No, I do not know what streetboarding is."

She snatched the papers off her clipboard and tossed them on the table behind her. Then she dropped the clipboard on the ground. "It's a board, bigger than this. And it has four wheels on the bottom." Then she leapt up, landing both feet on the clipboard. "You jump on it and kick your feet to make it move. Then you ride it down the street."

I felt my eyes widen and tried to correct. "While you remain erect?"

She nodded. Her knees bent slightly, she held her arms out, seemingly for balance. "Yeah, you stand on it. And you can do moves. Flipkick, ally, grate. I'm not the best, but I'm not terrible. Anyways, I was hurrying to get here, so I rode instead of walking and I ate it and wrecked my knee."

"You...ate it?"

She laughed. It was a brilliant thing. Like a lightbulb exploding. It almost frightened me. I had never seen anyone do that. A real thing like that. I only knew Iris's practiced laugh, her head tilted back, or Cacophony's rehearsed giggle.

"It's an idiom. It means I fell so hard that it seemed like I got some bits of street in my mouth."

"You must be in pain."

She shrugged. "I've had worse." She gestured to my hands. "And you obviously have had even worse than that." She peered at my fingers, moving closer. Her face was so unusual. Big, brown eyes with thick, dark lashes. Full eyebrows. But she did have all the right angles and symmetry. There were distinct ...mistakes. Her hair did not have a regulated curl pattern. It was part wavy, part straight. Some strands followed rules, and others didn't. And she wore it piled on her head in a big, swirly disaster. But I wanted to touch it. To explore it. So different than mine, which hung straight and black around my shoulders.

"Why did they do this to your hands?" she asked. "It looks so awful."

"It looks awful?" The fear in my voice could not be missed.

"I mean...I'm sure they will be perfect when you're all healed. But right now it looks...hellish. Why are your fingers mounted and all...disassembled like this?"

"The Grand standards of beauty change often. And so we must be adjusted."

She looked up at me like I'd said something wrong. "You mean, you weren't ill or injured. This is a completely preferential surgery?"

"Yes."

"That's the stupidest thing I've ever heard."

Smiling was not usually in my repertoire.

"Why did you hide your smile, Marrow?"

Someone who read my name off the chart rather than asking me. "It is not usual for me to smile. Not part of my particular beauty. Besides, it can create wrinkles."

She tilted her head. "I think wrinkles are beautiful."

"You are not a Grand. Your beauty logic is flawed."

She rolled her eyes. "I've met a Grand. And he was legit wearing a beak, hermano. They can keep their logic to themselves."

"Hermano?"

"Means 'brother'."

"What's 'brother'?"

She stared at me, shocked. "Do you know what a family is, Marrow?"

"I do not. Will knowing this make me more beautiful?"

"Oh my god"—she looked around, as if someone were watching us—"what the *hell* is going on here?"

Before she could say anything more, Hafiz came in and sneered at her. "Enough now. Time for Marrow's feeding and rest."

He shooed her, and I wanted to go after her, to tell her to come back, to tell me what 'hermano' was and 'family'. To show me more streetboarding. To tell me how wrinkles could ever be beautiful. To show me why some of her hair curled and some did not.

"I can still smell it," Hafiz said, covering his nose, though no scent lingered. "Grit shit."

He could say whatever he wanted about her. I had just experienced something for the first time. An actual conversation.

She thinks...I'm a person.

Ep 14

What Matters

I figured Helix was the person to ask. Iris and Cleft would make it about themselves. Cacophony was mildly unhinged. The twins couldn't take anything seriously. And Lavish and Muse filtered everything through hedonistic lenses. Gradience might have been helpful but they were not on a speaking day.

That left Helix. She was the coldest of us, even more so than me. At least I knew she knew how to think.

I was always unsure of how to greet her. She did not understand most customary things. She was lying on her bed, perfectly still, staring at the ceiling. Her dark hair had natural tints of blue to it and it sprawled out over her pillow in perfect, long, tight ringlets. Her brown skin seemed to hold every color in it.

"I have a question for you, Helix. Do you have time for me to ask?"

She hummed as she contemplated. "Do I have time?" She didn't look away from the ceiling, though there was nothing at all up there. Her voice was flat, monotone. Devoid of life but overflowing with meaning. "That is a good question, Marrow."

"No, no. That is not my question, Helix."

"So you have two questions for me."

"I suppose so."

"Come."

It took me a moment to understand her meaning. Then I crossed the room and crawled into the cot beside her, rolling onto my back without damaging my hands. The movement alone hurt intensely, but pain itself was familiar.

Wow. There really is nothing on this ceiling.

"Helix, did you have any interesting Grades evaluate you yesterday?"

"All things are interesting, Marrow. It's up to us to take interest or not."

"Yes. I see." I contemplated how to describe the last person to inspect me. She didn't weigh or measure me. She didn't pinch my skin or shine lights in my eyes. She didn't even ask me to walk for her. "Did anyone...talk to you, Helix?"

"They all spoke."

"No, did any of the evaluators actually talk to you. Like...as if you mattered?"

"Do you know what matters, Marrow?" Helix lifted a slender, poised arm above her and unfurled her fingers, pointing to the ceiling.

"I don't understand," I confessed.

"I know," Helix said with a sigh. "Matter matters. Are you matter, Marrow? Do you matter?"

"I don't know what you're talking about, Lix."

I twisted my head to see if my ignorance had upset her. But her face was unchanged. All angles and cheekbones, and not one hint of distress or concern or even curiosity. All of that she kept in her mind where no one could see. And I wished, as always, that I could understand what she did so she didn't have to carry it anymore.

"Don't wait, Marrow. They tell us we will live forever. But everything dies, in the end. Don't you see?"

I kept studying her face. "I don't see. Can you tell me?"

"I...am trying to."

"Would you like to come out with me, Helix? We could walk together, like we used to. I can't hold your hand today, but we can still be close. It might be nice. You can see the sky through the window. Maybe we can tell Gradience a story since they cannot speak today. Come with me. You can only stare up there for so long."

"That is what I am telling you, Marrow. You can only stare up there for so long."

I sat up. I could tell I was upsetting her. Or maybe she was just tired.

"Thank you for talking to me," I told her. "I know that's not easy for you."

She fell silent. Back to her spiraling thoughts.

I left the room. If Helix had met the girl with the injured knee, she would have remembered her. No one could forget someone like that.

Ep 15

Beyond You

Late again. I took the sharp corner with a bit more care. Flying off my board would not get me to the bus any faster. And the Glimpse I'd examined was very concerned about my scraped knee in our last session. I didn't want to increase his concern unnecessarily. I had other things I wanted to talk about with Marrow. So once I was in sight of that twelve-wheeled vehicle of mercy, I kicked off my board and started to run for it.

Didn't make it very far.

Someone grabbed onto the back of my shirt, tugging me backward and throwing me onto the ground. A man circled in front of me, standing between me and my ride out of Here.

"Where do you think you're going?"

Mervil. God, I hated Mervil. He smelled like tequila and sour milk and sleeping in his own mess. His patchy beard made me want to hit him.

"I don't have time for this," I said. It was true. I had to get on that bus. If I didn't, they would assign Marrow to someone else. Maybe even to that bastard Horatio. Or worse. They would kick me out of the program altogether.

"You'll make time for this, Mädchen." Mervil's red, bleary eyes could barely focus on me.

"What do you want so I can tell you I don't have it? I gotta go, man."

He squatted down to where I still sat on the street and put a dirty hand on my sneaker. "Your hermana was short last night."

"Don't touch me." His hand on my foot made my whole body go hot and cold at once.

"That better not be what your sister said last night." He pulled, so he could grab my ankle, the skin of his palm now touching the skin of my leg, making my whole body seize in disgust.

I tried to get away, to yank my leg from him, but he squeezed tight and pulled harder, the force dragging me across the street toward him, so he crouched over me. I looked around, hoping someone would take notice, but the only people watching were three or four of Lăobăn's guys backing Mervil up.

"We have quotas," Mervil said. "Do you know what that means?"

"I know what quotas are, Mervil, and I also know what your *Mutter* would say if she knew you had your hands on me in the middle of the street in broad daylight." She lived on our block. When we were kids, she made strudel for anyone who finished their chores on time. But pastries couldn't save her son from the life he chose to live. From Lăobăn.

Mervil laughed. Every time I saw him, it seemed he was missing more and more teeth. "You're going to tell my mother on me, little girl?"

"Yes."

And he swallowed but didn't back down. "Tell Confía she's falling behind." He slid his hand up my calf. "Unless you want me to tell her myself."

"What is going on here?" Cyrilus stood erect, the sun shining harsh and casting a brutal shadow over us.

"None of your business. Grades don't run these streets."

"No," Cyrilus said. "Grades would never use our hands for brute force, as you are doing now. They are instruments of measurement."

"I'll use my hands however I want," Mervil said, and he dug his nails into my calf hard enough to make me gasp.

"The person you are assaulting is under my jurisdiction. And my need for her supersedes yours. Release her at once." Cyrilus' eyes flashed as he peered down. "She is beyond you."

Mervil sneered. "She'll end up right where she belongs, old man. Beneath me."

Calmly, almost in slow motion, Cyrilus reached his hand out and put it on Mervil's shoulder. Immediately, Mervil released me. He said not another word. Only got up and moved aside.

"Let's not be late, Bellanueva," Cyrilus said.

He offered me his hand and hoisted me to my feet.

"Are you injured?" he asked.

"I'm alright." I looked back over my shoulder. Mervil stood without moving or speaking. Like a dummy.

"What did you do to him, Cyrilus?"

"I measured him," he replied, as if everyone should know what that meant.

I dusted myself off as we walked back to the bus, trying to hide my slight limp. "Am I in trouble?"

"You are not," he said. "And with your latest scores, it is not very likely that you will be released from our service any time soon. You have nothing to worry about, Bellanueva."

I had plenty to worry about. But that was irrelevant at the moment. "You can call me Bel, by the way."

He nodded. "And you may call me Cy. But only when we are off duty."

"You have an 'off-duty' version of yourself?" I tried to imagine Cyrilus with a t-shirt, smoking a blight and sipping a beer.

"There are many versions of me, Bel. But for this version, we will remain formal."

I thought for a second, looking Cyrilus over as he oversaw loading students onto the bus. He sported more liver spots than I thought possible. Balding, gray beard. Not exactly a party animal.

"Thank you," I said, before I got in. "Genuinely. I would have missed the bus if you hadn't come over."

He nodded. "Perhaps one day you will return the favor."

In the back seat of the bus, I plopped down next to Mango, looking forward to unwinding and taking in the scenery. She grabbed my hand as soon as I sat.

"Oh my god, are you okay, Bel?"

"Me? I'm alright."

"There's no way you're alright. I would be in tears if I were you. Sobbing. Freaking out. That awful man tried to hurt you!"

"Mervil sucks. But he's not *that* scary. There's much worse out there."

"What did he want?"

I shrugged. "Long story."

Mango sighed. "You're full of long stories that you never tell, huh?"

I inhaled, still holding her hand. "They sleep my sister out for money. She came up short. That guy wanted me to deliver a message to her. See? Long story."

Mango's eyes were wide. "This is *normal* to you? Good lord. Where do you *live*?"

"East West. Dime Block."

"Oh." She got real quiet, real fast.

We rode in silence, which was fine with me. I didn't know how rough it was where Mango lived, but there was nowhere like Dime Block in all of Here. I expected her to treat me differently once she knew. Most people did. Put some distance between us. We were all Grit, of course, but Dime Block was grime.

Still, Mango surprised me. For the whole ride to There, she didn't let go of my hand.

Ep 16

Basic Empathy

I tried to be less frazzled while walking into the room. I didn't succeed, but I tried. I sat down on the chair, forgetting it swiveled, and had to do a full rotation before I could face my subject again.

"Hey, Marrow," I said, using my sneakers to squeak to a stop. "How are you today?"

Marrow. How to explain this human? Better start with the eyes. They were the darkest I'd ever seen. Almost no pupil and iris differentiation, except for the tiniest slivers of reddish-gold so fine that I thought I imagined them. His skin was so smooth and firm, it looked like it was carved from clay. Straight, dark hair that floated down around his broad shoulders. In many ways, he looked like he could have been the first human ever made.

His mannerisms were the most interesting part. Everything was detailed to perfection. When he moved, he told a story. How he tilted his head. How he raised his hand. It was all so...holy. Reverent. Deep.

"How am I?" he asked.

I loved his voice. It sounded like purpose. Something I wildly wanted but could never actually grasp. It could never be mine. No one could possess a sound.

"How are you? Like...how are you feeling?"

His eyes darted whenever he didn't understand something. I didn't bother to take notes on those sorts of things. Marrow was easy to remember.

"I am feeling strong. And well-positioned," he responded.

I chuckled. "That's good. But I mean...how are your emotions? And what do you think about your position with regards to recent events? That's what I mean by 'how are you'."

"I see," he said, pausing to think. "I apologize for my lack of understanding."

"You don't have to ever apologize for the way you understand the world. Not with me."

He met my eyes. I tried not to blush. He truly was the most beautiful thing I had ever seen.

"So...how are you?"

He nodded slightly, making his hair swish. *He smells like black pepper and tree bark.* I wished I could bring a handful of his hair to my nose and just breathe.

"I am feeling...glad."

I smiled. "You are? That makes me so happy."

His eyes darted. "My gladness makes you happy?"

"Of course. That's basic empathy."

"It sounds dangerous."

I frowned, leaning in. "Empathy? Dangerous?"

"If I feel what you feel, I might react as you react. What if I smiled as you did? Or frowned as you are now? I could wrinkle. It could cause imperfections."

"And that would be dangerous?"

He lowered his voice to a whisper. "They might remove you. If you were to mar me."

"Remove?"

"I would not see you again. They would terminate your role."

I sat up straight, my heart pounding. "They would...kill me? If I made you smile?"

"Highly probable."

He took a breath to steady himself. No one would have noticed unless they were paying as much attention as I was. He was nervous. It did not show on his face or even his eyes. But the breath told all.

"Besides," he continued. "I am permitted to smile. But it is very costly. One day, a Grand will pay great costs to see it."

I narrowed my eyes. "How much we talking, hermano?"

"I have heard Hafiz say 10,000 gol for one look."

I stuffed my hand into my pocket and pulled out a fistful of soggy, crinkly gol. "I got four right here." I wanted to pass it to him, but his hands were still not operational. After hesitation, I decided to tuck it into his shirt. We were close then. My knuckle grazed the skin of his chest. It was much cooler than I expected, and goosebumps pricked where I'd accidentally touched. Awkwardly, I sat back down and tried to pretend I was a normal, sane person. "What will that get me?" I asked.

A natural smile tugged at the corner of his mouth. I almost had a legit heart attack. It was the most enchanting thing I had ever beheld.

He glanced down at his shirt. "What am I to do with this?"

"Keep it. You earned it."

His eyes flicked over to me, hovering over my leg. "Your knee. It is healing." Then, he leaned forward. "What are these bruises on your leg?"

"Oh?" I tried to hide my bruised leg behind the other. "A little mishap."

"Looks like a handprint."

I shrugged, ready to move on. But Marrow was not ready.

"Someone hurt you. Why?"

"These things happen," I said, trying to stay calm. "What's most important is that I grade your beauty correctly. If I can do that, I might become an actual Grade. And you will get to be an actual Glimpse."

"Do they hurt you to teach you how to Grade?"

"No, Marrow." I paused, thinking back to my last test ."Well...they didn't hurt my leg, if that's what you mean."

He exhaled. "But they hurt you in other ways?"

"I suppose. But it's to teach us to think."

"They hurt us to teach us to be beautiful."

We both sat quiet for a while. I studied his hands, how each had been sliced into and stitched back up. They were braced with some sort of mechanism to stabilize them and keep them from fine movements.

"Are you medicated right now, Marrow?" If so, it would have affected how I measured his beauty. And my report was due soon. If I measured it well, I would move on in the program. I would be closer to becoming a real Grade.

"I am not," he said. "It is not permitted when I'm due for an evaluation. I must remain mentally sharp. Or I may not present myself properly."

Another long moment of silence. With me staring at his hands and him focused on my ankle. Then Marrow broke the hush. "On our first day, we are each told a story. Of how we were made. That story is what makes us beautiful." He stared into my eyes, a deep well that could draw anyone in, maybe forever. "Knowing that will help you Grade me."

"You are not supposed to tell me this, are you? Glimpses are not supposed to advise Grades. And especially not students."

"I am not supposed to tell anyone ever."

I shook my head. "Then don't tell me any more. I don't want you to get hurt, Marrow."

"They will hurt me either way." His expression did not change, but his eyes darkened. "That will always be true for me. But it does not have to always be true for you. I will help you...."

"Bel. You can call me Bel."

"Bel," he repealed. "Meeting you is so much gladness for me."

I chuckled. "Nice to officially meet you too."

"Is it really? Nice to meet me?" His eyes searched my face. I could tell he was holding his breath as he waited for my answer.

And that's when I decided that helping the Glimpse named Marrow was the most important thing I would ever do.

Ep 17

Shut Up, Cacophony

There were no windows where we lived. The sun could have damaged the skin. Caused blemishes and discolorations. Because of that, sometimes, if we were lucky, one of us would grow faint from lack of exposure to the light. When it happened, we would be taken on a walk. Or be allowed to sit on the roof until we regained some strength.

On the day my hands were healed, I decided to grow faint.

It was tricky. Too weak, and Hafiz would have me intubated in a medical bed. Not weak enough, and I would be sent to my cot for a moment of rest. I had to make it clear that it was sunlight I needed. That no other remedy would do.

I spent most of the morning shivering. Just a little. And glancing at the window when I did so.

"What's wrong with you?" Iris asked as she glared at me during stretches. "You look so sickly."

I ignored her. And then shivered once more.

"Seriously," she said, stretching beside me but staring at my form the whole time. "What's wrong with you?"

"Maybe he needs a...*deeper*...stretch," said Lavish, bending inappropriately, his tongue flicking out at me. He ran his hands through his short curls and winked the bluest eyes. I often wondered how he did not utterly exhaust himself.

"Maybe he's dying," Cacophony said, with a giggle. His golden hair stuck out in many directions on his head. But he was perfect. A god chiseled from marble with the eyes of an imp. "We could have him removed! Put him out of his misery."

"Shut up, Cacophony," Iris said, scolding the other Glimpse. She tossed her purple hair. "He's not dying, he's just fading. Beauty doesn't last, they say. Poor, poor Marrow.

Wonderful. All I needed then was to make the slightest groan when I reached my arms up. I began to catch Hafiz's attention.

And then, on the second-to-last step of the routine, I forgot my footing. Stumbled. Which I *never* did. I was known for my grace.

Hafiz was at my side in a moment. "Are you unwell, Marrow? This won't do. It won't do at all. The Grands will not have it. You are to be debuted soon."

"I am fine," I insisted. "It's only a slight chill in my joints."

He tsked and ushered me toward the door. "Go to the roof and rest for a while in the sunniest spot. The sun is not so harsh right now. Come back down when you feel revived."

"Yes, Hafiz. I will not stay in the sun too long. I know the dangers. If I am still stiff, I will move to the shade and rest."

This pleased Hafiz. He smiled, opening his bejeweled eyes wide. "You are so considerate, my Marrow. Truly the prize of my work."

I climbed the stairs to the rooftop alone and stepped into a flood of sunlight. With my newly lengthened fingers, I grabbed onto the ladder that ran along the side of our home. It was there in case of an emergency, though I could not imagine anyone in all of There using such a thing as a ladder.

I was a bit nervous. *What if I fall? I will become all scraped and bruised. I will be ruined.* But then I pictured Bel, with her banged knee and her bruised leg. She had fallen. And she was not ruined. When she smiled, everything around her became beautiful. And if she could be brave, I could too.

So I managed down the ladder and set my feet on the streets of There. Unwatched. Unfollowed. Unminded. For the first time in my life.

Now...how to get to Here from here.

Ep 18

Not A Day Later

The streetlights buzzed. The ones that were still working did, at least. Not much functioned on Dime Block. East West of Here was where broken things went to die. Dime Block was where dead things went to have some fun.

I missed dinner—again—and I knew Confía would have questions about where I kept running off to. But I couldn't tell my sister I was testing out of Grit. Not yet. I still had time to imagine her being happy for me, wrapping me in a hug and telling me to spread my wings. Imagination was better than what would really happen. I'd break her heart. And she'd be left to earn twice as much.

But I would promise to send gol back home. And I'd earn more than Confía ever could. Maybe enough to buy our way out of our mess. To build a home for the little ones. To get out of Dime Block. There were better places Here. I'd heard North of North was decent. And Southern Tip was basically There. Someplace like that where the kids could play without stepping on glass or slipping in car oil. Someplace where a half-decent fence was enough to keep men out at night.

I rounded the corner for home in a hurry, as always, and for the second time in one week, someone reached out and yanked me by the back of the shirt.

My cursing fit was cut short by a hand clamped over my mouth. I watched as my board rolled without me down the cracked sidewalk and was immediately scooped up by some kid in a dark jacket.

I elbowed whoever grabbed me, and he folded like wet laundry, releasing me to clutch his ribs. Beneath a black hood and silver-rimmed glasses was Ratio.

"What are you *doing*?" I punched his shoulder, mostly because I thought punching anywhere else might have actually killed the skinny punk. "You followed me home? Are you actually trying to *murder* my family, you psycho?"

"No, I was just trying to sound tough," he said, trying to coddle both his shoulder and his ribs at once. "Look." He pointed toward my house.

I was in too much of a rush to realize we had company. Several armed guys, guns in hand, stood at the bottom of our steps. And a few more waited near the pearl-white car that sat on our street. A car everyone in East West recognized as the ultimate sign of a bad day.

Lăobăn. In our house.

My unfiltered reaction was to sprint in there and get my family out, but Ratio tugged me back again.

"Are you crazy?" he hissed, ducking behind a parked car and taking me down with him. "What are you going to do if you go in there, Bel? Huh? Punch them all in the shoulder?"

"I can't stay here and do nothing," I hissed back. "And why are *you* here? Are you with Lăobăn?"

"Yes," he said, deadpanning. "I rolled up with the most notorious Grit crew in all of Here, and then I snuck behind these cars to tell you not to go inside. And during my days off, I moonlight as a Grade in training. Just for fun."

"Why are you *here*, Ratio?"

He jabbed his thumb over his shoulder. "I live a few streets over."

"You're from East West? No, you're not. I would know. I would have seen you before."

"I've seen you a million times."

"Where?"

He gestured to my house. "Your house. School. Testing. Everywhere. I've lived here my whole life. You wouldn't have noticed. I keep to myself."

"So do I," I argued. "And you noticed me."

"Of course I noticed you. You're Bel De Leon. You are terrible at keeping to yourself. Also, your sister's a legend."

I pointed my finger practically into his nose. "What are you about to say about my sister?"

He put his hands up in mock surrender."She's a legend. That's it."

"That'd better be all you say." I turned back to the house, to the men outside with the guns and the scowls. If I spent the time, I could recognize each one and recall where they lived and whether they still lived with their mothers. "What could he want? Lǎobǎn?"

"I have no idea."

But we were both playing dumb. We knew what Lǎobǎn wanted. And how. And when.

Me. On my back. In 98 days. And not a day later.

Ep 19

He Walked

I waited until the pearl-white car drove away. Ratio said he would wait with me, but that dedication disappeared around hour three of us lurking, knees bent, beside the parked car on our street. So I kept myself company, daydreaming about the strange clock on the ceiling of the Grand Tower. And about Marrow and his hands and if they were healed. And whether Grades had found another part of his body to mess with, and what I could ever do about it.

Once all was clear and the guns had been packed up, I decided to go home the back way, through my neighbors' yards and over their dilapidated fences. There was way too much drama still lingering on our front steps. The meanest thug in East West often left a stink when he took off.

The back way was cluttered with abandoned cars, overgrown shrubs, and huge chunks of misplaced asphalt. For those reasons, plus the alarming lack of streetlights, the path stayed pretty untraveled. I had the way memorized though. Which crates not to step on and which tree limbs would hold my weight when I scaled certain areas of the fence.

"Bel?"

Hearing my name called out in the darkness threw me. I skidded off the beat-down car I was climbing over and rammed my knee into the fence I was supposed to hop.

"*Dios*, who is that?" I asked, picking myself up off the ground and examining the damage to my elbows and knees in the dark. "Are you trying to scare me to death?" I squinted in the low light, trying to make out the voice. "Ratio, you turd? Is that you?"

"What is a turd?"

I gasped. Really, that was an understatement. It was more like...my whole heart stopped. It didn't go cold or hot or numb. It stopped.

"Marrow?"

He stepped forward, and the closer he got, the more of him I could see. He wore what used to be a white shirt. It wasn't cut in a style I'd seen on anyone in Grit. The seams were nuanced. Odd. His skin was so flawless, it glowed, even with the lack of light.

"What? What...*what*?" I couldn't say anything else.

"Are you afraid?" he asked. "Have I frightened you? I did not mean to." He paused, his eyes darting. "Perhaps I should go."

I forced myself to find something to say. "How...are you...*okay*?"

His eyes twinkled at that. "You always ask me the same question."

"It's an important question."

He tilted his head, stepping even closer. "You are the one who seems not to be okay."

"I...." I pulled the elastic band out of my hair so I could rub my scalp and get blood flowing to my brain again. "Is this some sort of test? Who brought you here, Marrow?" Glimpses did not wander through Here. Ever. Yet here one was.

"No one."

"No one? How is that possible? Do they know you're here? The Grades? Your caretaker?"

"They do not."

"Then...how did you get here?"

He observed me so carefully, with eyes that took in every detail. It was one of a thousand reasons why he was so out of place, standing among garbage in the dark on Dime Block. Grits did not look at each other carefully. We looked at one another like we were starving and maybe one of us was hiding food in our pockets.

"I walked," he answered. "I asked for directions whenever I got lost. It took some time to get Here. I am sure Hafiz is looking for me by now."

I stepped toward him. "Marrow, you walked from There to Here? That must have taken hours. You could have been hurt. You could have been *killed*."

He nodded. "I did not know that when I set out, but I am aware of the dangers now. There were many."

"So you're not alright. Oh *Dios*." I rubbed my chest. My heart was definitely not stopped anymore. It raced, banging against its cage. "I might actually be sick."

"Bel...."

I smacked my hands together. "Marrow, what were you *thinking*?"

He didn't answer. But I found the sadness growing in his dark eyes.

"I'm sorry I'm yelling," I said. And I was so sorry. He didn't know why I was so upset, why the thought of him coming all this way was nightmare-inducing rather than a wonderful surprise.

That's when, without being able to stop myself, I reached out and touched his elbow.

Now, I knew—*I knew*—I was not supposed to touch my subject. It was on every Grade test I had ever taken. *We can't study something if we manipulate it. If we handle it. If we hold it.*

But my hand on his elbow led to him leaning into me. He wrapped both arms around me and put his cheek to my hair. And he lingered. In his still, slow way.

I clutched the back of his shirt and pressed my face to his chest and fought the tears that came to my eyes.

"You're okay," he said calmly, with that voice that sounded like magic being born. Like a fantasy opening its eyes.

That was the first time I realized how much everything hurt, all the time, from every direction, and how much I wished it would all stop.

Everything, that is, except for a Glimpse named Marrow.

Ep 20

Roadtrip

"What are you...*doing*?" Marrow asked, still holding me close to him. His heartbeat was steady and even, though I was certain mine was still blaring.

I sniffled, the cloth of his shirt muffling my voice. "What do you mean, 'what am I doing?' *You* hugged *me*."

"Forgive me, Bel, but I don't know what that means."

I pulled away, just enough to look up at him to see if maybe he was just playing the shitty comedian. But he seemed just as serious as always. I was beginning to think perhaps Marrow couldn't tell a joke. Maybe he only ever told the truth, straight up, no chaser.

"You don't know...what a *hug* is?" I asked. *How could a human being make it this long without knowing what that means? Without giving or receiving one?*

He shook his head, his long hair swaying around his shoulders.

Wonderful. Not only did I touch him, and without his permission, I have now molested him. I let all-the-way go, then, and stepped back. " I am so, so, so sorry." I slapped my hands to my cheeks. "I'm probably embarrassed enough to drop dead right now."

"Please do not do that," he said, moving toward me. "Please."

I thought he would leave it at that, but he became visibly anxious, clenching and unclenching his fists, his breathing accelerating.

"Hey, hey. No," I said. And I rubbed his arms. Because that's how one person was supposed to calm another. "It was just a silly expression, Marrow. I'm not going anywhere. I'm not actually going to die."

"People are removed because of me all the time."

I blinked. "Oh." I shook my head, trying to clear it. Trying to make it turn on. Like banging a tele set to make the picture come through. "I'm sorry. People die Here often as well. I guess I make it seem funny so it isn't scary."

"Explain the hug," he said, changing the subject.

I grinned. "You put your arms around someone to show them you care about them. It helps them feel better." I waggled my eyebrows. "Did you like it?"

With his chiseled face, in all his solemnity, he said, "It is the best thing that has happened to me so far."

I blushed so hard. "A hug?"

"Hugging you."

I choked, and my throat made a gurgling sound against my will. I smoothed rather sweaty hands on my jean shorts.

"Um...so...what are we going to do with you? You really, really can't stay here. If Grits knew a Glimpse was walking around Dime Block, they would make a piñata out of you. And I don't think you're storing any candy in that torso, hombre."

Marrow blinked. "What?"

"They'll beat you with sticks until your insides come out. It's a game kids play at parties."

His eyes widened. He looked around as if the stick wielders were lurking behind junk piles. "And you live here? With the people who beat these children?"

"No, no, no." I sighed, pulling my hair back up into its bun so my sweat didn't glue it to my neck. "Okay, never mind that. The point is, we need to get you back home. Immediately."

"I don't want to go back, Bel."

"I figure wherever home is probably sucks, Marrow, but this is not better. Trust me. This is crazy dangerous."

He nodded. "I trust you. Of course I trust you." Then he shrugged his perfect, broad shoulders. "I could walk back."

"Did you not hear anything I said before?"

"Oh, right." And then he grinned. "The piñatas."

I chuckled. "That was funny."

The grin turned to a smirk. "I thought so."

"Well then," I put my hands on my hips. "Road trip, Marrow. Time to steal a car."

Ep 21

No Permission Needed

I worried that Bel might trip and fall as we made our way over debris in the dark, but she seemed to know where she was going. I was not supposed to worry, though, and the realization that I worried made me do it even more. In a way, I could see why Hafiz taught that we should avoid such mental exercises. They degraded minds, and thus bodies, quite quickly. *How long does it take to form a wrinkle?*

We made it to a street, and even though it was late and we Glimpses ought to have been sleeping—or pretending to be—people and cars walked about loudly.

"There's an old lady up the way," Bel said as we went. "She hardly ever leaves home. And she has an old car she doesn't really use much. We can jack that."

"Jack it?"

When Bel walked on the streets near her home, she was different than she was during our interviews. Her eyes opened wider, her nostrils flared, and her posture stiffened. She was alert. Always looking. Probably for whomever wanted to beat me like a piñata child.

"Jack it. Like...take it without permission."

"Could we not ask permission?"

She scoffed. "She'll say 'no' if we ask."

"Maybe she'll say 'yes'."

"She won't. She hates me."

"Is that why you chose her car?"

Bel smirked. "Maybe a little. She liked to call the Guard on my brothers and me when we were kids."

She walked up to a maroon car and tugged on the door to a compartment at the back of it. The door opened, and she held a finger up to me.

"You be the lookout."

"What am I looking out for, exactly?"

"For anyone who suspects what we're doing."

"And if someone suspects?"

"Just...be cool."

She gestured to me, and then ruffled up my hair. "No Grits walk around like newborn gods. Could you just try to be less...ethereal?"

"I have spent countless days trying to be *more* ethereal. Now you want me to stop?"

"Yeah. Look worse. You stand out too much when you look this perfect."

I had no idea how to look worse. So I stood still and tried not to try anything at all. *Maybe that will make me seem better at being worse.*

Bel braced her arms and the back of the car and hopped, lifting her legs and then her whole body into the compartment. Thudding noises as she kicked a barrier on the inside of the compartment. Then the barrier gave way, and she crawled through. A click, and she opened one of the front doors and came back around to where I stood. She slammed the compartment door closed.

"Get in," she told me.

"But you just closed that compartment."

She smiled, her eyes glittering, her nose dewey, and her cheeks flushed. "There are doors on both sides."

"You look different," I said, going around and pulling the handle on the door. I sat down in the seat and pulled the door closed behind me.

"I do? How so?" She slid into the seat across from me and pulled a panel of wires from the undergirth of the car. She fiddled with them, only half listening to me.

"You look...more alive. And radiant. Your skin and eyes are glowing."

She flashed me a grin. "That's the adrenaline."

"What is that?"

She sat up as the car engine roared to life. Then she put her hand to her chest and wiggled her shoulders. "Feel-good hormones your body makes."

"They make people look beautiful?"

Her cheeks reddened even more. "I guess it depends on what you think is beautiful."

"There's only one beauty." I straightened up in the seat. For posture. "That's what I was taught."

Bel edged the car into the street and took off, glancing at the mirrors that hung above us. "Whoever taught you that is full of shit."

"What's shit?"

She stared at me. "Umm...it...it's the stuff that comes out of your butt after you eat."

"Oh. I've never eaten."

Bel whipped her head to face my direction. "What did you just say to me?"

I shrugged. "I have never eaten. Why? Have you eaten?"

"*Yes*, Marrow. I wish I could do it every day, of course, but I do what I can. Eating is *wonderful*." She put her attention back to the road. "They don't feed you

There? I know for a fact that there's food. I had a berry once."

"I am nourished through a tube."

"Oh my Dios, so you must be starving right now. Marrow, you're probably dehydrated!" She smacked her hand on the wheel that she used to turn the car. "I'm going to kill a Glimpse. Then I'll be fired. Then I'll die. This cannot be happening to me."

"Why are you so upset about my nourishment tube, Bel? Why are you talking about dying? Are you joking again?"

She sighed. "No, I'm not joking this time. Life is complicated in Grit, Marrow. And you being Here makes it more complicated."

I nodded, trying to keep still even though I wanted to jump out of the car. "I am sorry. I was selfish to come."

Bel rubbed her temple. "It's okay. You weren't selfish; you were reckless." She looked at me, her brown eyes making quick assessments. "Why *did* you come all this way, Marrow?"

How to explain. "I...couldn't be There anymore. And the only thing I could think of that made me feel...not There...is you."

She stopped the car and leaned her head back against the seat. The sun was coming up, spreading gold along the edges of her hair. “I don’t know what to say.”

“That’s alright. I *never* know what to say.”

She grinned. “Come on. Get out.”

I looked out the window. Nothing appeared familiar. We were clearly still Here. “But…we are not back yet. Why have we stopped?”

Bel winked. “Tacos.”

Ep 22

The First And Last Bite

I handed the very last of my gol to the pissed off woman in the filthy apron behind the stained counter, and she almost slammed my fingers in the window when she shut it.

"She seems very unhappy," he said. Someone else would have frowned, but Marrow's facial features rarely moved. Like he were chiseled from stone. If that stone were flawless, glowing amber skin.

"Most people are profoundly unhappy Here," I explained.

"Then why do you stay?"

I sighed. "Because...getting out of Grit is almost impossible. There's no way to become a Grand. Best chance is to be a Grade. And that's unlikely since our education system is designed to make us compla cent, not competitive. We have to teach ourselves if we want to excel. And everything about our lives is designed for that to be an impossible feat."

"Yet you are nearly a Grade, correct?"

I nodded. "I'm lucky, I guess."

"No. Lucky would have meant you were born a Grand. You are not lucky; you are determined."

"I'm desperate is what I am."

"Because you do not want to work behind the glass like that sad woman who took your gol."

Because if I stayed in Grit, my fate would be worse than Taco Lady Linda. I thought back to my family, to the guys with guns outside our house, and my stomach tightened into a hard knot.

"We sit and wait now," I told Marrow, trying to distract myself. "Better do it in the back, though, since you look like an angel."

"The smell is interesting," he said, his eyes watering. "What is it?"

"Onions. And beef. And queso. Just wait, you'll see."

"I was told food was an...oral experience?"

I slid into the booth and patted for him to scoot in next to me. "You'll taste *and* see."

"So...." He looked around. "What is this place? Do you have more than one home?"

"No, this is a restaurant. It's just for eating. People gather to share meals. It's a thing we do with people we like."

"You like me?"

I chuckled. "Claro que sí." I put my feet up on the empty chair across from me. "Or else I wouldn't share a meal with you."

"And this cost you gol."

"Sure did." I elbowed him. Touching was becoming more natural, though it still made my heart beat faster. "You're worth it, though."

The tacos came out and they sat before us in all their glistening, greasy glory. "Go slow," I warned him. "Your stomach and jaws won't be able to handle much. This is mostly just for tasting."

"I just...put it in my mouth?"

I modeled for him, taking a big bite out of one of the tacos and chomping.

He lifted his—gracefully, which was no surprise—and bit into it, the shell crunching and splintering.

He sort of froze, like the most elegant statue. I thought for one terrifying moment that I'd broken him. *Maybe Glimpses can't eat.*

"Marrow? You okay there?"

His eyes began to water. He set the taco down and left the booth, the door ringing after him.

I grabbed the food—leave no taco behind—and followed him, setting them down on the hood of the car so I could catch up to him.

"Marrow, stop. Wait." I grabbed his arm. "Talk to me. Are you okay?"

"No," he said, shaking his head. "I am not okay, Bel."

I rubbed his arms like my sister always did with me when I was anxious. "What's wrong? What are you feeling? I can't help if I don't know what's going on."

"I want to go back."

"Back...to my house? Marrow—"

"There. To Hafiz. To the other Glimpses."

I nodded. "Oh. Okay, then. Let's...um...let's go."

I tossed the tacos in the back seat for later, and we drove in silence. I was familiar with the way There, but I had no idea what to do once we arrived.

"Can you find your way if I park up at Grand Tower?" I asked as I pulled to a stop in front of the enormous pillars.

Without a word, Marrow got out and walked into the Tower. He didn't even look back. Not once.

Ep 23

Where All The Ideas Go

My home was not as I had left it.

Guards scoured the Tower, their boots scuffing the elegant flooring. Furniture had been upturned. The stretching room was empty and sealed off.

Cacophony, of all Glimpses, saw me first. He twisted his long neck, his enormous eyes narrowing with delight. But delight for Cacophony was usually not delight for anyone else.

"Marrow, Marrow, Marrow. You have returned to us at last."

"Where is everyone?" I asked. "They should be stretching."

Cacophony inhaled with a hiss. "All activity is halted, Marrow. They are searching all over There for you."

"Why would searching for me keep you all from your regimens?"

"Because," Cacophony slithered toward me, his languid body and long limbs moving like a serpent's. "You are the one they can't afford to lose, darling. The most beautiful. And now...the most interesting." He was close enough to trace his smooth finger across my chest, around my shoulders and back, walking tight circles. "Where did you go?"

"Walking. And I got lost."

"Of course you got lost. None of us have ever gone 'walking' alone before. Why did you leave us, Marrow?"

"Because I wanted to walk." I shrugged my shoulders to get the Glimpse off of me. "Where is Hafiz?"

"Soiling his pantaloons in distress." And Cacophony laughed at his own joke.

A joke. That is what Cacophony and Iris used to amuse themselves so much. I had never been introduced to jokes since I was not a Glimpse who was made more valuable by smiling. And all my life, I'd wondered why some people could burst into laughter when there was no reason to do so.

But Bel made jokes. And she taught me. And I learned. Her jokes did not hurt people, like Cacophony's did. They were meant to make things easier.

To help. I decided that whenever I chose to joke, I would do it like Bel. For better, not for worse.

"You smell...strange..." Cacophony said. He put his nose up to my face and inhaled. "What is that? It's awful."

"I will find Hafiz," I said, walking away from the Glimpse.

The hallways were ransacked. Every bench askew. Even the art that was meant to depict us was removed.

I knocked on Hafiz's door, but no one answered. I stood there for a while, knocking, yet there was no response.

"He is indisposed."

I turned. Helix stood there. Her dark blue ringlets were loose and unbrushed. Her brown skin still held a myriad of colors, but it was not as moisturized as was customary.

"What does that mean?" I asked her. "Indisposed."

"Perhaps you will open the door and see for yourself," she replied. She stared at me without needing to blink. It always made me nervous. But her tear glands had been adjusted so that her eyes did not need to shut as often. It led to many sleepless nights for her, but her chilling beauty was rare and exquisite.

"Helix...what is going on? I left for not even one day. Why is everything destroyed?"

She sighed and gestured at me with her perfect hand. "You are not destroyed now, are you?"

I sighed. "No. I am not." I looked around. "Are you saying this is my fault? I am why the Grades are not testing and Hafiz is not tending to us?"

Helix might have smiled if it were permitted for her. "Did you have an adventure?"

I took her hand. "Yes. I did, Helix. And I have come back to tell you all that there are such things as adventures. And that jokes can be helpful. And that food is not what we were told it is."

She stared down at her hand in mine. "What are you doing?"

"I...." *What am I doing*? "I don't know."

"Release me."

And I did. Touching Helix did not feel the same as touching Bel.

"What do you think all this is for Marrow?"

"The food and the jokes?"

"No. The Grands. And the Grits. The Glimpses and Grades."

"I...have no idea."

"Hmm," she said. "Marrow has no idea." And then she turned to leave. "That is because I took them all."

I shivered, unsure of what to do next. Finally, I decided to open the door, to confront Hafiz, to tell him that the world was better than he had taught me and that I wanted to live, even if it meant I could no longer be beautiful.

But when I opened his door, Hafiz did not spring up to greet me. His legs dangled, a foot off the floor, and his body twirled in the oldest dance. His face was bloated, his glistening eyelashes brushing swollen cheeks. The bedsheet around his throat was knotted tight.

So this, then, is what Helix meant by 'indisposed.'

Ep 24

I Can Always Come Back

I was not stupid enough to drive Old Lady Abernathy's car back to her house. She'd be waiting, no doubt, ready to turn me in. So I left it just outside of East West and walked the rest of the way.

The sun coming up in Grit didn't necessarily make it a more pleasant walk. The heat made the piles of garbage reek and allowed the maggots to force their way into full-fledged flydom. The trick was to walk fast. If I slowed down, the flies confused me for nesting ground.

I wanted to take the rest of the tacos home for the familia, but neither the insects nor the neighborhood mooches would let that happen. I stopped just long enough to hand the box to a couple of kids who were looting a receptacle for breakfast.

They didn't thank me. Only snatched the box from my hands and ripped it, shoving the food down their throats faster than the flies could find it.

I licked my fingers, savoring what was left of the taco grease.

The closer I got to Dime Block, the more nervous I got. Nothing was really out of place except for the way people looked at me. Most people knew who I was. One of the De Leon girls. The weird one who kept to herself and didn't have the curvy hips that Confía did. But still, a De Leon girl. My mother had left us a decent reputation.

I was used to the occasional nod as I walked through, not staring and muttering and complete silence as I approached those who loitered in the streets.

By the time I made it to our street, I was all but running. My heart rattled my chest so hard, I thought it would burst through my body. Up the stairs. Threw open the door. It was quiet.

"Confía!" I called out. It was never quiet at my house. Always some child crying. Always my brothers cursing or brawling, breaking everything we borrowed—because honestly, we owned very little.

My sister came out of her bedroom. She propped herself up in the doorway, her fingers gripping the frame. Her sleeve hung off her shoulder. Bruises lined her neck and colored her face.

"Confía...what happened?" I moved toward her.

My older sister shook her head and put her hand up. "Don't come any closer," she said.

"Fi, why? What is going on?"

"Where were you last night, Bellanueva?"

I inhaled. Of course I couldn't tell her about Marrow. It could put her in danger. There were rules. "I saw the car out front. I waited outside—"

"Bel, the truth. Right now. Where do you keep running off to?"

"I...." I took a shaky breath. "I took a test. And I got a perfect score, Fi. LIke...*perfect* perfect. I knew I would break your heart, so I waited to tell you. But...I'm in training to be a Grade. That's where I keep going. To the Here Center. And, Confía, I've even been There! I've met Grands and Glimpses. I wanted to tell you everything, but...."

She nodded, wiping her nose with the back of her hand. "You think you're good enough? To make it?"

I nodded. "Fi...I'm really, really good."

"Alright. Then get out."

I stared. My whole body, my fingers and scalp and legs, went cold. "Confía...what is going on? Lǎobǎn did this to you? He can't just come here and beat the shit out of you whenever he feels like it. We have to *do* something."

"Yes," she said. "We are doing that something right now. You are going to take a few of your things, and you are going to leave this house and never, ever come back. No matter what."

"I'm not leaving you, Confía. You're my sister."

"I am *your* sister, Bella! And so you will listen to me. Mom is gone. Dad...dad is gone—"

"Gone? What do you mean—"

"He is *dead*. Dead. And I...I am stuck. But you, Bel? You have a shot. You have a way out. You are going. Eyes forward. No hesitation."

The tears released themselves. "You can't make me leave you."

"I will never forgive you if you don't go." And her voice growled, like the words were coming from her soul.

"If I go—if you make me—I'll come back."

"No. Never. Promise me. Swear it."

My hands shook. My brain couldn't decipher between thoughts. Only a reverberating panic pervaded. "What if I need you?"

Confía laughed. And even though her black and blue eyes were filled with tearful spite, she was so beautiful. "What you need from me, is what I am doing for you right now. You will not step foot in this house again. And you will not visit. You will not send gifts. You will not even hug me as you go. Just. Leave."

I gathered the few things I had, though I could hardly see past my emotions. Fear. And rage. And then fear again. I took a couple outfits, the note Mom wrote me when she left, the knife dad gave me when I turned 4,800 days old, and the books I'd stolen—as many as I could carry. My whole life in one bag.

When I revisited the kitchen, Confía was not there. No one was.

I was alone.

Ep 25

Fair Game

If there's one thing I knew better than to do in East West, it was wander. If people found out I had no place to go, they'd know I had no one looking for me to come home. Bellanueva Anamaria Morales De Leon would be fair game, and no one would even know I was gone.

So I went north, headed for North of North. By the smell of Mango's clean clothes, I had a feeling she lived there. I didn't expect her to put me up, but I hoped maybe I could ride with her to the Here Center on the mornings we were to report for training.

The air was fresher the further north I walked. And there were a few trees. I forgot how much I liked those. The big branches shaded me from the sun, and the bark calmed me when I rested my palm against it. Little breaks. The bag was cinching my shoulder, and the seams along the bottom threatened to tear. And how I wished I had my streetboard.

About halfway there, I realized I hadn't eaten in two or so days, except for the bite of taco, and I hadn't slept either. My bones hurt, and my brain was begging for a decent cry. Since the flies were less villainous, I decided a rest would have to be taken.

I found an older building with less traffic than most and pulled a hoodie out of my bag and over my face. I kept my knife in my hand, slumped to the ground, and closed my eyes. I stuffed the bag in my hoodie to keep it safe and admired the way the brick wall could hold its own, no matter how many Grits took naps leaning on it over the years. I told myself, as I drifted off, that I would prove Confía right. That I would pass those Grade tests and make it. I would live There and eat berries and thank her everyday for forcing me to leave. This I told myself. But I no longer believed it.

It was a good spot. I made it until evening before someone kicked my sneaker and I peeled groggy eyes open. Part of my heart hoped it was Confía with an apology and a hug. And the other part wanted to see Marrow, with his deep eyes and smooth skin, ready to try a burrito this time.

But it was Mervil. Still stinking of sour milk and tequila. And probably down a few more teeth since the last time I saw him.

"Get up," he said, kicking my sneaker again. "Let's go."

I clenched my knife even harder. I said nothing. Only tried to get my body to calm down so I could think of what to do.

"I said get up," he repeated, kicking even harder.

When I didn't respond and didn't move, he reached down and grabbed the front of my hoodie, hauling me upward.

I let my legs go limp, so I fell out of his grasp and to the ground. I scrambled, hoping to make a run for it, but Mervil's shoe connected with my ribs before I got very far. After the third kick, which made a sharp crack through my torso, I curled up into a ball. So as to not die.

I lost my knife, but Mervil had not been close enough for me to use it. So I had to bide my time, counting down until he eventually got tired. Then I could find the knife, do what I had to do, and run like hell.

"Waste of my time," he grunted, spitting on me and then grabbing me by the ankle so he could drag me to whatever car he had waiting.

But he stopped. And he stared at me with wide eyes. And then he fell with a thud to his knees. And then he flopped over on top of me.

My knife stuck out of Mervil's back. And standing there, with deep eyes and that smooth skin, was Marrow.

Ep 26

So...Not Okay

"Marrow!" I called out to him as he stood still a few short lengths away. "Are you alright?" Mervil's bleeding body crushed me in place. I strained to get out from under him, but it was no use. Dead men meant dead weight.

Marrow didn't move. Or speak. He didn't even blink.

After a few attempts, I managed to slide myself out from under my attacker. One full inhale was all it took for me to tell my ribs were broken. I stumbled to Marrow and took his hands. They were ice-cold. I rubbed them, one at a time, to get his blood flowing again.

"Marrow? Marrow, you're in shock. It's okay. You're okay." I said these things to him over and over. "Can you breathe for me? You're holding your breath right now. I need long, slow exhales."

I modeled for him, and eventually he emulated, breathing out for ten seconds, in for four, out for ten. The same way Confía taught me when I'd gotten anxious as a child. It never failed to calm me down, even after our mom left. Even after our dad drank more than he spoke.

Finally, warmth returned to Marrow's fingers, and his eyes flickered.

"You're okay," I told him once more.

"No," he said. "I'm not. And you're not. We're not okay."

I tried to swipe the blood dripping from my nose with the back of my hand so I seemed more normal, but it only increased the flow. I really hoped my voice wouldn't tremble when I spoke, but it usually did whatever it wanted. "We're going to be okay."

"Killed him."

I looked at Mervil's body, face done on the ground. *Yes. We killed him.* And that meant Lăobăn would find out. He would put the pieces together, realizing that Mervil was sent to retrieve me and never returned. He'd hurt me. And if he couldn't find me, he'd hurt Confía. *But what to do? What to do?*

"Mervil didn't give us much of a choice, Marrow," I said. "You helped me. It's going to be fine. You'll see."

Marrow shook his head. “No, no. Hafiz. They killed Hafiz.”

“Your caretaker? He’s…he’s dead?”

“They killed him.”

If that was true, why was Marrow Here? The Guards should have been sorting through the issue. The Grands should have wanted to protect the Glimpses. The Grades should have been measuring and calculating, making sure the beauty of the Glimpses remained unaffected. “Who? Who killed him, Marrow? Was Hafiz removed? Did he do something wrong?”

Tears filled his eyes. And I had to admit, though I hated myself for it, that there was nothing more horrifically, tragically beautiful than the crystal tears that ran down the face of a Glimpse.

“The others. Helix. Cacophony. Iris. The Glimpses. They killed him.”

I reached up and put my hands on his cheeks. “Marrow, did you have a bad dream? That can’t be true. It just can’t be.”

He placed exquisite hands on top of mine and looked into my eyes. “They hanged him from the ceiling. I know he did not do it himself, Bel, I know this. Even if he was devastated that I ran away. God Across knows that Hafiz enjoyed being Hafiz. More than he enjoyed cultivating my beauty. More than he enjoyed anything. He would never...."

"You need to report it. Who can you tell about this, Marrow? Who helps you, besides Hafiz?"

He shook his head. "I don't know what to do. It's always been Hafiz. Always. Only."

"Who does he answer to, then?"

"I don't *know*, Bel." He inhaled. "I don't know anything. And I don't understand what is happening. Why...why was that man trying to kill you?"

"He wasn't trying to kill me. He was going to take me away. To force me to work for him."

"But he kicked you. So hard. So many times. I thought you would die. Like Hafiz. And then...where would I go? Who...who would look at me fondly? I would have no one. I would be alone."

I put my arms around his waist. "I won't let you be alone, Marrow."

"I killed. And they killed. We kill."

"You're not a *killer*, Marrow."

"I killed. I removed. I remove. I am someone who removes."

I looked up into his face, trying to understand what was happening. Whether he was still in shock. Or whether it was something else. Something worse.

"We need to get out of here," I said. "I'll take you home, and we'll figure this all out. I can tell Cyrilus, my teacher. He'll know what to do. He'll help."

"I have a car," he said, sniffling.

I balked. "You...*drove* here? You can drive?"

He nodded. "I drove here, but I don't think I should do any more of it. I watched how you did it the last time. Through the back and connecting wires. And I copied your movements. I hit many things on my way here. Even some people." He paused. "I wonder if I killed them, too."

"No," I said firmly. "I'm sure everything is fine."

We held hands, but I had to let go, just for a moment, to run over and pull my knife out of Mervil's spine. I wiped the blood off on his pants. And then, because Dime Block ran through my veins, I patted his pockets and scored fifty gol and a piece of chocolate.

I exhaled, regaining some composure now that we had some sort of plan. I wiggled the chocolate bar so Marrow could see. "Splitsies?"

High time to teach the Glimpse about emotional eating.

Ep 27

A Murderous Freak

Oops. Little details escaped me. Like the fact that I was covered in Mervil's blood and accompanied by There's most ethereal Glimpse as I walked to the car that Marrow stole to get Here.

"People are staring," I muttered under my breath, trying to keep a low profile by moving as casually and quickly as possible.

"Is that not the usual way of people? Staring?"

"Not for me," I told him. "You're used to being looked at. It's new for me. And they aren't staring because I'm supernaturally beautiful. They're staring because I look like a murderous freak."

"How could you look murderous if you did not murder? I am the one who should look murderous."

"Let's stop saying the word murder or any derivatives of that word, okay?"

Marrow stopped and pointed to the ground beneath his feet. "I left the car right here," he said. "I'm sure of it."

I wrinkled my nose. "Was it a really pretty car, 'Row?"

"I thought it looked nice."

"Yeah, someone jacked the car you jacked."

He nodded. "Like murdering murderers."

I yanked the elastic out of my hair and let the waves fall over my face. Then I pressed my hands to my eyes. "This is fine. This is great. I just need to steal a car, go There, figure out who's responsible for Hafiz's death, restore law and order to a harem of the world's most beautiful babies, and then figure out how to evade certain death while saving my sister from the result of my mistake. Oh, and then show up for Grade training and pass my tests."

"Tacos."

I smacked my hair out of the way. Marrow struggled to open the candy bar wrapper. Then, he smelled the chocolate. "This smells different from tacos." He put the whole thing into his mouth in one bite and made a gurling, gasping noise in the back of his throat. "God Across," he said. "What is this?"

"Chocolate. It was invented to please the Grands. And I see you have yet to learn the rules of 'splitsies'."

He smiled, chocolate smeared all over his white teeth. "It is very different from tacos. Both are good."

"Doesn't the food hurt your stomach?"

"Yes, very much," he said, licking the wrapper.

I sighed. "Let's start the search."

"What about the man I murdered? The one who I stabbed with the knife? Does he not have a car?"

I tilted my head. "A couple notes, 'Row. One, I remember exactly who Mervil is and what happened with the knife. You don't need to keep bringing it up. And two...that is brilliant. Let's go. I know exactly what we're looking for. He stole it from one of my brothers last year."

Buckled snuggly in the car we stole from the guy who stole the car from my brother, who stole it from someone else, we started on the road to There. I picked up arepas from a stand on the way, happy to spend some of the money we took from the corpse's pockets. He wasn't the corpse of primary concern, though, so I tried not to spend too much time thinking about him.

"You should stop the car," Marrow said once we were speeding through open fields, with no one around.

I did, and he got out and climbed onto the top of the car. I followed him, about to swallow my last bite of arepa, still sipping from the bottle of guava nectar I'd splurged on.

Marrow looked out at the sky and the span of land and shrubs that separated Here from There. He took a swig of nectar. "This liquid," he said, "makes me wish I could go up."

I laughed. "Most people call it juice."

"But it is indeed a liquid. So I am not actually wrong." Then he paused. "Bel? Do you think I could be smart one day? If I tried to? Even if it did not increase my beauty?"

The sun was busy turning the sky pink and blue and purple and gold. I slipped my arm around his waist and leaned into him. He put his arm over my shoulder and swayed into me.

"Marrow, you are already smart. And you're brave. And kind."

He took another sip. "I've never needed to be brave before I met you."

I bit my lip. "I'm sorry...."

"No," he said. "Don't ever be sorry for giving me a life, Bel. I never wanted one before I met you, either."

Ep 28

We Have To Go Through

One hundred percent sure I was not supposed to go into the behind-the-scenes portion of Grand Tower. But there I was, in my bloody shirt and ripped sneakers, standing in front of an open door at the very back of the gaudy building.

"We have to go through," Marrow said calmly after I stopped moving altogether. "That is how doors work."

"I know how ordinary doors work, Marrow. This is not an ordinary door."

"It shares the same function as all doors I have encountered so far, I can assure you, Bel."

"But I'm not allowed in there."

"I have seen you do many things you aren't allowed to." To demonstrate his point, he laced his fingers into mine. "When our palms touch, I feel

certain about things that I was unsure of before. So I will hold your hand, and we'll go through."

I took a deep breath. "And we can fix whatever is broken in there. Everything is fixable."

Marrow opened the door and led the way. I expected a blast of shimmering light, glitter to rain from the ceilings, scented walls, floors that let you hover over them rather than sullying the soles of your feet. After all, Grand Tower was magnificent, with its diamond windows and a clock that kept counting down to zero with not so much as an explanation. It made me even queasier the second time I saw it. But I noticed that Marrow hadn't even looked up. Just walked straight to the door as if he was accustomed to the scenery.

But once we were past the threshold, the space behind the door was...ordinary. The walls were painted cream. The floors laden with square, white and black tiles. The ceilings were low—no domes or arches, no diamonds or marble. The whole place was plain. Sterile.

And destroyed.

Furniture lay in broken heaps in the hallways. Since there were no doors to any of the rooms, I could see that the cots had been flipped and thrown around. Some were even wedged in the window sills.

In a large room, it was clear that mirrors once covered the walls. But all that remained of those mirrors were enormous spider web cracks and shards of reflective glass. The pieces of mirror on the floor were reminiscent of glitter but not the sort I'd expected when entering the home of the Glimpses of There.

"Where is everyone?" Marrow asked. His voice was thick, as if he spoke past a lump in his throat.

"Where would they usually be at this time of day?" I asked, squeezing his hand tighter.

He shook his head, his hair—more matted than usual—swishing around his shoulders. "This is all wrong," he said. "Hafiz should be here by now. We should be stretching and practicing our walks. And tomorrow, we will have one-on-one consultations with the Grades, so we should need extra rest. For our beauty. And he will hate how much I am worrying. Hafiz does not like it when I worry."

I rubbed the grooves of his knuckles with my free hand. Of course, my stomach tightened so sharply I had to fight the urge to hurl on Marrow's shoes. *How could he have forgotten about Hafiz?* Perhaps the shock was worse than I thought.

"Let's find them," I said. "They have to be here somewhere."

But Marrow began inhaling more often than he exhaled. "I don't understand," he said, his eyes wide as he observed the shattered mirrors. "I don't understand."

"You're okay," I said. The panic was contagious. But I shoved it down. Along with the pain in my ribs and the dread in my stomach when I imagined someone finding Mervil's body and reporting it to Lăobăn. "You stay right here, Marrow. I'll see what I can find."

I let go of his hand.

Down a few more hallways, a room that was larger than the rest. I knew it was special since it was the only one with a door. Inside, a strange, unattractive smell. Putrid, really. Not exactly the scented walls I'd imagined. And a man I'd seen only in passing, his brown face bloated, his swollen tongue bulging from his gaping mouth, dangled from the ceiling.

I did vomit then. Arepas and guava and a bite of taco.

By the time I pulled myself together and returned to the room with the mirrors, Marrow was gone.

Ep 29

They Can't Just Ignore Glimpses

"They want him now. And with haste."

I awoke to a dozen or so Grades bustling around me. Usually, Grades moved with precision, all their calculations done beforehand. But nothing about this was usual.

"You will have to open him," one Grade said to another as they flitted about in their white coats with their white masks, though one of the two was barely holding on to his. It dangled from an ear, and he did not take the time to fix it.

"We cannot simply open him, Cyrilus," the unmasked Grade said. "Where are the plans? Where are the roadmaps?"

"There are no plans and roadmaps today. Still, it must be done. The requirements have changed. And today they want to see him. Will you be the one to tell them we are not ready? That they will have to wait another century?"

The unmasked Grade sighed. "It must be done."

They spoke to each other as if I were not present. This I was accustomed to. But on every such occasion, Hafiz was present to explain to me how I ought to adjust myself to the adjustments. How I ought to think of myself going forward. So I could better add the pain to my beauty. But Hafiz was not there, and this was not alright.

Where could he be besides here with me? Grades adjusted Glimpses one at a time. He was with each of us as he read our charts to the Grades. He ensured they operated well. He ensured we were not marred.

With Hafiz not present, who would ensure these things?

"I want to go home," I told the Grades. But when I tried to sit up, I realized my arms and legs were strapped to the table they'd stretched me out on. This, again, was very normal for larger, more intensive operations, specifically involving major organs or muscle groups. Sometimes, deeply set bones. But it did not feel normal.

"Let me out," I said, yanking on my restraints. "Where is Hafiz? Let me out. I want to see him."

The Grades ignored my request. *This is not right. They can't just ignore Glimpses.*

"Bel?" I remembered her. Like a light through haze. "Bel. Bel. The girl. She is a Grade. She can explain to you what I mean. She gets me food and shows me fields. And she holds my hand. Let me see her. She will find Hafiz for me."

"You should gag him," the Grade named Cyrilus said to the other. "Or we will lose our focus."

So they can't hear me. "No," I said even louder. "No, no. Listen to me. Something is wrong. Something is very wrong. I am afraid. And fear will decrease my beauty. I do not want to be afraid. Please."

But another of the many Grades put a strap into my mouth and covered it with a mask. It was more difficult to breathe, as the material covered both my mouth and nose. Still, I tried to cry out.

"Sedation?" the unmasked Grade asked.

"There is no time. Sleep will come after the pain."

Where is Hafiz? Where is Bel? And the other Glimpses? Where have they gone?

"Clavicle and breastbone increase," Cyrilus said. "Easy healing, so do not touch any joints. And for the love of God Across, someone address his hair

and skin. And void his intestines. They are bulging. Now. Do it now!"

The Grade named Cyrilus leaned over me, the operation light a halo around his covered head. He raised a scalpel. "And someone find me the Grade in training. Bellanueva Anamaria Morales De Leon. 71.89 days old."

Ep 30

It Meant No Harm

"Open your eyes, Marrow."

I don't know who said this. When I obeyed the command, I found no one in the room. I was no longer bound to an operation table. Instead, I was standing upright. There were no visible signs of the surgery I'd endured. No narrow incisions, no rows of stitches. No bruises or swelling. The only evidence was mine to bear.

The pain of having my chest opened and then clamped shut again. The deep, deep ache of being dismantled and carefully but rapidly reassembled.

The darkness in the strange room was cut only by a soft orange light. I had never seen a light source like it. Though each step was agony, I felt myself drawn to it. It did not glow steady like a bulb. It...breathed. A living light. And it was not only orange. I saw this as I moved nearer. It held yellow and blue. The faintest purple when it turned and twisted just right.

Slowly, I put my hand out. I thought, with great sorrow, that Helix would love to see this...this light. She would sit and stare for many days. The closer I got, the warmer my hand felt, and the more it shone against my amber skin. Until I touched the beauty.

I forgot that beauty is not to be touched.

The light leapt up to my fingers and seared my flesh. Every cell in my body screamed in terror. I gasped, which made my chest burst with pain, stumbled backward and away from the light.

That is when curtains I had not noticed lifted. The surrounding darkness shattered, and brilliant bulbs flooded the space.

What seemed like a thousand people stood outside a flawless glass stretching from the ground to many lengths over my head and curling into a dome. These people...they were not like the Grades and certainly not like Bel. They reminded me of Hafiz, if Hafiz were preparing to eat me.

Some had slits for eyes and licked out extended forked tongues, though they stood as tall as any man. Others had necks so long and thin that their heads barely balanced on top of them. I saw one whose eyes were plastered shut, yet still they stood facing me as if they could see through their bondage. One looked like a bird, with a beaked nose and beady black eyes, feathers growing from its head and neck and shoulders.

I held my stinging hand, unsure of what to think or what to do. I wanted to run. I wanted to run. I wanted to run.

And so I tried to. I scrambled forward, my heart tearing at my unseeable surgical wounds. I put my uninjured hand forward, feeling the glass for any type of door or window. Any vent. A way out.

The light in the center of the room still burned as if it was not evil, as if it meant me no harm. Perhaps it had only been protecting itself. I was a stranger after all, and it was I who tried to touch it, not the other way around.

Maybe it could help me, this light, if I asked. There was no way out. And the only way I could keep checking for an escape was to go closer to the people who stared without speaking, just outside the glass.

I walked back to the light to ask for its aid. I decided I would touch it again, that maybe it would be kinder the second time.

But as I reached my other hand out, this time with it quivering and not on purpose, I heard a voice shout my name.

"Marrow, don't!"

And I don't know where she came from or how she got into the glass dome or why. But Bel ran toward me and pulled me back from the light and into the shadows.

Ep 31

Conversations About Conversations About Conversations

I wished there was a way for my brain to comprehend what was happening. Or at least for my body to process it well enough to produce the right chemicals for the correct corresponding emotions. But it appeared my body was doing everything wrong. Fear felt like sadness, and worry felt like pain, and I just wanted to go home, but I didn't have one anymore.

The Grade questioning me was relentless. The same inquiries over and over. "Why are you There? Who brought you into the Tower? How many days are left? What did you Glimpse?"

The last one was their favorite apparently. Every Grade asked it more often than the other questions, and with varying inflections each time, as if the way they said it would change how I might answer. But my answers were always the same.

"I don't know what the hell you're talking about. You can't just keep me here. What do you mean 'how many days are left'? And where is Marrow?" Sometimes I peppered in a little, "If you're hurting him somewhere, I'm going to burn this place to the ground."

The Grades found me just after I found Hafiz. Not one made any mention of the used-to-be-handsome brown man dangling from the support beam. And I knew I was supposed to be finding help for Marrow, letting the Grades know that he needed someone to take care of him, but I didn't want to talk about Hafiz, or the lack of him. I wanted the memory of his bloated body removed from my mind.

The Grades "escorted" me out of the Tower and to a room in another building—one I recognized because I'd used it before. To talk to Marrow when we first met.

In their white clothes and masks, the Grades seemed bothered. Hurried. Almost panicked. They sat me down and began questioning. Multiple Grades came through, one at a time, with their

clipboards and their confusion. *Is this what it was like for Marrow? A barrage of useless inquiries and people looking right past you, trying to find some answer?*

"What is going on?" When no one answered me, I stood up. If they were going to ignore me, only using me for their dumb analyses, then I'd leave. Screw them. Screw the whole thing.

"Sit down, Bellanueva."

Cyrilus entered the room, his mask removed, clipboard in hand. The other Grade who'd been questioning me left without a word. The old man and I were alone in the room. He sighed and sat in the chair opposite me.

"What is going on?" I asked him.

"Why don't *you* tell *me*?"

I inhaled, clasping my hands together to help me stay calm, and then exhaled. "So many things."

"Let's start with Hafiz."

My stomach dropped. "He...seems dead."

"He *seems* dead?"

"I mean...." I shrugged, but I wanted to vomit again. Good thing I was starving and there was nothing left to hurl. "I didn't like...check...or anything. But from a cursory glance, I'd say yeah. Pretty dead-ish."

"And you were the one who killed him?"

I almost fell backwards out of my chair. "What? Me? No! God no! What?"

"So you did not?"

"I am saying to you with as much clarity as humanly possible, *no*. I did not kill Hafiz."

"Then who did?"

I blinked. "How would I know this?"

"I thought you might."

"Well, I don't."

Cyrilus nodded. "Why are you There, Bel?"

I chewed my lip. I knew keeping it up would make it raw, but I chewed it anyway. "I came to help Marrow."

"Where is Marrow? Aren't you supposed to be helping him?"

I looked around the room, which was silly because he wasn't going to simply appear due to wishes and stomach rumbles. That wasn't how people and appearances worked. "I let go of his hand to check on Hafiz. And then he was gone. I'm assuming you have him. And if you do, just know he didn't do anything wrong."

Cyrilus nodded, eyes abnormally large behind thick spectacles, his liver spots multiplying with each day we lost. "What is wrong, Bellanueva?"

"Like...what's wrong? Or what is the *definition* of wrongness?"

"Both."

That's when, with a sudden burst of realization, I knew that Cyrilus had no intention of returning me to my previous life. That I would not become a Grade. I would not be someone who got to ask the questions. I messed up. And from then on, I would be the one to whom the questions were asked.

And how did I know this?

Because...I never got a "goodbye" from my mother. Instead, she left me a note. One that I stuffed into the bag that sat in the back seat of Mervil's stolen stolen car. One that I would never see again.

> *Dear Bella. This will be the last thing I ever say to you. So pay attention. Bel. You're not wrong. Love, Mom.*

Ep 32

Grit Presentation

"Cyrilus," I said, trying to calm myself, trying to sound reasonable and intelligent. Hoping to convince myself that I actually was all of those things. "Please, be straight with me here. Is this another test? You said I was beyond this. Beyond being pushed around and treated like Grit. Treated like trash. At least do me the decency of telling me what kind of trouble I'm in."

Cyrilus sighed, setting down his clipboard and pulling off his white mask. "Bel, alright. I will tell you. But you must promise to continue with the Grade program. You must promise to help us."

I nodded. "All I've ever wanted is to be a Grade."

"It's Marrow," Cyrilus said. He took the white cap off his head and rubbed gloved hands over his scalp. "He is...."

I sat up straighter. "What? What's wrong?" My eyes pricked with tears. "Is he hurt? Is he dead?"

Cyrilus shook his head. "No, Bel. He's...beautiful."

I blinked. "Uh huh." *Festers and fleas, what is this crazy man getting at?* "I know he's beautiful. He's a Glimpse. That's why we've been studying him. To increase his beauty metrics."

"You don't understand," Cyrilus said. "He's more beautiful than ever. More beautiful than he should be."

"How...how can that"—if I picked at my fingers any longer, I'd bleed, but I couldn't help it. "What does that mean? More beautiful than he should be?"

"His increase in beauty is sudden. And unprecedented." He leaned forward, resting his elbows on his knees. "Do you have any idea how long we have been studying Marrow? How often we have incrementally increased his beauty? It is very difficult to alter. It requires minor adjustments over time. Do you know how long this has taken?"

This was a common, entry-level Grade testing question. "Forever," I said. "He was never born, and he won't ever die."

"No."

I sat up even straighter. "*No*? What do you mean 'no'? That's the first thing we're taught about Glimpses. Everyone knows this."

"It's not exactly correct. You see, we tell people we have been studying them forever. But we only say this because we don't know how long it's been."

I gestured to the clipboard he'd set down. "Just check your records, hombre."

"We can't. I mean...we do. We have. But we still don't know."

"The records go on forever?"

"The records are gone."

"Gone. Gone where?"

Cyrilus sighed. "They're gone, Bellanueva. They *go*. Now tell me, what did you do? To increase his beauty so drastically?"

"I didn't do anything to Marrow."

"You'll do it again." Cyrilus jabbed his pointer finger into his knee. "There. In front of us all. Where we can see it."

"Do *what*?"

"Increase his beauty."

"I didn't *do anything* to increase his beauty."

"You're wrong."

I clamped my jaw shut. *Wrong. I'm not wrong. I'm not.*

"He will be with the Grands soon. And they will want to see this increase as it occurs. In real time. You'll be brought to him, and you'll do it in front of them. We will watch. We will measure. And then we will understand."

"How will you understand? I am trying to tell you that I don't understand what you even mean."

"What do you say to him? To Marrow? When you are together?"

I threw my hands up. "I don't know! Just normal things. Everyday things."

"Give me an example."

"Hey, 'Row, maybe I should drive from now on."

Cyrilus made a choking sound in his throat and reached for his clipboard again, pencil poised. "He drove?"

I shrugged. "He told me he did, so yeah."

"And the name you called him? 'Row?"

"It's just a nickname. Like Bel instead of Bellanueva. Or Cy instead of Cyrilus."

"He responds to it?"

"Of course he does. Why wouldn't he?"

"A Glimpse only responds to his given name."

I tilted my head. "Given name? Who names them?"

"We...don't know."

I nodded. "Ah. I bet that just 'goes' too, huh? What do you know, Cyrilus?"

That hit a sore spot because the old man got up and left without another word in my direction.

But to the Grade who opened the door for him, he said, "Prepare her for the Grands. Grit presentation."

Ep 33

A Buzz And A Clank

The Grades took me to an empty room and tied me to a wall.

That was the first sign that things were not about to go my way. I didn't need to rely on instincts to come to that conclusion. It was obvious at that point. My arms splayed out, a sense of extreme vulnerability washed over me, turning my stomach into a knot of fear.

"I want to go home," I said very loudly and clearly to absolutely no one.

Lights flashed on. But to call them lights didn't describe them well enough. They were blazing. So bright that I screamed and shut my eyes, and still they burned through my eyelids. But worse was the way they seared my skin. I could feel the heat start to peel my nose and forehead, and my forearms sizzled. Blisters bubbled almost instantly.

With a buzz and a clank, the lights shuddered back off.

Then, a particularly large Grade came in, wearing his white garb. He balled up his gloved hand and swung, colliding with my right cheek. I felt my head flop backward, cracking against the wall. He struck again, and my nose shot pain up into my head, blinding me yet again. He moved to open hands then, slapping me in my face, on my arms. Finally, he kicked my legs, bruising my shins and thighs.

I yelled for them to stop. I called for Cyrilus. For anyone to put an end to it. To at least explain why I was being punished this way. But no one explained.

I waited and waited, my wrists hanging from their constraints. Then, I slumped back against the wall as best I could, but there was no way to rest, to lie down, or even to sit.

"Drink this." It was the most anyone said to me in hours. A female Grade, by the looks of her build, held a small vial to my lips. I took it without hesitation. I would have drunk anything.

I would have eaten anything. If it meant I could go home.

But it wasn't water. And it sure as *hell* wasn't guava nectar. The flavorless liquid stung my mouth and throat. But worse than that—worse than anything at that point—was what it did once it hit my stomach. It seemed to suck all the moisture out of my body, pulling it away from my muscles, my skin, my brain.

I groaned, and hearing that groan scared me. Because it sounded like I was dying. It was, in all truth, the noise a dying person makes. I didn't want to die. Most of life had been spent trying to avoid that very thing.

I begged. But no one listened.

Finally, because nothing lasts forever, a Grade appeared with a bucket in hand. He chucked its contents at me, and I choked and gagged, inhaling fine particles of...*dirt?*

Yes. I knew the smell, the taste. It was dirt. Ordinary, plain, unassuming brown dirt. Though, strangely enough, it smelled like Dime Block. Like piss and used cigarettes and the last dregs of old liquor. I gagged. Then, terror took hold of me. *Why does it smell like Dime Block?* I imagined Grades flipping through a catalog of scents, curated for Grit, and choosing the one I belonged to. *This is my smell*, I thought in a creeping panic. *This is what they want me to smell like.* I imagined my own face and body, blistered and bleeding and bruised. *This is what they want me to look like.*

I wheezed, blood and dirt in my mouth, my body trembling from dehydration. I understood, at last, what they were doing. And why I could never go home again. This was no happenstance. This was no accident. My life was not a series of ill-fated transactions and misdemeanors. My life was on purpose. Just like Marrow's. Just like Confía's. And Mervil's. And my mother's. "Grit presentation," Cyrilus had said. There was someone—something—they wanted me to be.

I am Dime Block.

Ep 34

The Lights Never Look Like That

It wasn't until Bel put her arms around me that I knew I was naked. And cold. And afraid.

She was clothed at least, though the fluffy overcoat she was wearing was covered in dirt, torn, and burnt. I could smell the smoke on her.

She held me, pressing her face into my chest, which forced me to cry out in pain. Immediately, she released me.

"You're hurt!" She looked up at me, keeping herself at a distance.

I moved to her and held her face in both my hands as delicately as I could manage. Her skin was swollen and blistered. Her nose bent out of shape, bleeding down her lips and chin.

"Who...did this to you?"

She wept in my hands, holding on to my wrists, too unsure of my injuries to embrace me again. Her eyes remained wide, alert as she looked around us. "We have to get out of here," she said. Her voice was thick and slow, slurring as she spoke.

I looked around the strange arena, the Grands watching with wider eyes than Bel's. "I don't know how. But don't worry. Hafiz will come."

"Marrow," she said. "Don't you remember? Hafiz...he's *dead*."

Dead? How could that be? He's always been There. Always been There. I shook my head. "Impossible. He'll come."

She sniffled. "We need to get out of here."

"There is no way out. Until they are finished, I suppose, with whatever this is." My eyes were drawn to the flickering light once again. "What is that? Do you know?"

She turned her head to it. "It's fire. You can't touch it, Marrow, it'll burn you."

"I've been burned before. The lights never look like that."

A sob escaped Bel, and she doubled over. She did not enjoy talking about the burning lights.

After a few moments, she straightened back up, pushing her hair out of her face. "I need to think," she said. But shoving her hair out of her eyes only served as a distraction. I had seen her change her hair to help her think before. When we stood outside of her house and she decided to take me home. When she began interviewing me the first time we met.

"Come," I said to her. Her arms were too sore to hold up long enough to wrap her hair. And though it was excruciating for me to lift mine, I could not think of a way out like she could. So I would bear the pain, and she would bear the thinking. "Let me."

I took her hair in my hands—it was softer than I ever imagined, all brown waves and curls every which way—and twisted like I had seen her do. I had nothing to tie it in place, so I tucked it in tight and hoped it would stay.

It did not. Her hair sprang out of its place, spilling over her face.

She laughed at that, even though she cried. It made me smile.

A hundred gasps from the Grands watching outside the glass.

The gasping startled us both, but then Bel snapped her fingers. "Gasps," she said. "That's how we get out."

She kicked her shoes off. Then she tried to lift her coat over her head, but groaned instead. I had forgotten about her cracked ribs, about the man I'd killed with a knife. How his body lay on the ground behind a filthy building.

"Help me take it off," she said, wincing. "Rip it if you want."

And so I tore her coat off her and helped her step out of her pants. She took every item of clothing off until she was as bare as me.

I tried to concentrate on what she was doing instead of how she was doing it, with her breasts free and her hair down around her shoulders. Even with the bruises and scrapes, I could tell her skin would be soft to touch, smooth and easy. It made my stomach hurt to think of testing that theory, moving my palms along her body.

"Marrow, stay with me," she said.

I felt heat rush to my face. "It is...distracting."

"If I can focus with a literally perfect naked Glimpse beside me, you can focus too. Everything hurts, and I need...to lie down...soon. We have to keep going...."

I helped her over to the flickering light, carrying her clothes and shoes in one arm, supporting her with the other, trying not to tear my entire sternum apart.

She squatted, holding her shirt over the light. It loved the shirt and began devouring it. Bel set the shirt aside. Then she did the same with her pants, her shoes. Until the light grew four times in size.

"Stand back," she said, and we hobbled away. She pointed upward, and I noticed the domed top of the glass structure filling with gray and white haze. "Smoke."

"This will let us out?"

"Either the smoke will choke us to death, or the Grades will have to get us out of here. Those are the only two options in the scenario I've set up."

"What if they don't let us out? What if they just want...to watch?"

"Then...I guess they get what they want. And they watch."

Ep ~~4~~ 35

Someone Would Hug Me

"Bellanueva Anamaria Morales De Leon. 7,379.42 days old. Born Here, not There?"

My knee bounced uncontrollably when I was nervous. That, I expected. But what I did not expect was to be sitting in a plastic chair in the Here Center, just outside the testing rooms. The bookwatcher clickety-clacked on her computation device.

"Bellanueva De Leon?" she called again.

That was me. I knew that was me. Just like I knew I was not supposed to be where I was, doing what I was doing. I reached my hands up and touched my face, feeling for blistered skin and bruises. I probably would have screamed right then and Here if I were all healed, if there were no trace of what had happened when my hands were bound to a wall and a Grade pummeled me until I couldn't stand it anymore.

But it was all there. The evidence. The gash above my upper lip and the dirt settled into the creases around my nose. All accounted for.

Where is Marrow?

My intent was to jump out of my chair, but the pain in my ribs only allowed me to creep to a stand. I hobbled over to the bookwatcher's desk, and the increase in inhalation made me cough. I hacked and hacked, aware that my lungs were seared and filled with smoke, but so confused that I couldn't pull it together.

Smoke, smoke. There was so much smoke. Where is Marrow?

"Are you De Leon?" the woman asked. "You're late."

Isn't she going to comment on how terrible I look? Ask me if I want a medic? If I need to see a Grade? I gasp-hacked. That was it. *Genius.*

"I need to see a Grade," I wheezed. "It's an emergency."

"You'll miss your test if you don't hurry," the bookwatcher said.

I shook my head. "What test? I'm not supposed to be taking a test. I need to find Marrow. I need to find him. I *have* to find him. Do you understand? We were in the glass cage with the Grands. They were staring and staring, with their beaks and their balloon heads. And he was naked and scared. He burnt his hand, and they burnt my face. I burnt the clothes; everything was burning. I need to find him, he needs me."

The bookwatcher adjusted her glasses, nearly lancing a ginormous mole off her nose. “Listen, honey. People get nervous all the time. These tests, they’re hard. It’s a lot of pressure for a Grit. It is. But if you take a few deep breaths, I bet you’ll calm right down and get in there before you run out of time. Because, honey”—she leaned closer and whispered—“*you are running out of time*.”

My eyes filled with tears. “A...test? I can’t take a test right now.” My inhale shook my body, and I pointed behind me, as if she could see what had happened in the past. “My sister...she made me leave home. I lost her. She’s gone. My dad’s dead. Hafiz is dead. And we killed Mervil. The Glimpses...they’re gone. And Marrow now too. Everything hurts, and I just wish someone would...would hug me and tell me what the *hell* is going on.”

“Let me ask you something, Bel,” the bookwatcher said. “I can hug you right now, and you can cry in my arms. Or—and pay attention to this part—or you can get that half a pencil out of your pocket and go take your fucking test. Which is the right choice?”

I blinked like she had slapped me. Then, because I didn’t know what else to do, I turned and walked into the testing area.

“You’re late,” the proctor said. “Take a seat and connect the electrode device please. Quickly.”

I pressed the sticky patches to my skin, wincing with each movement, even the subtle ones. None of the trainees seemed to think anything was strange as I looked around. Mango focused intently on filling in answers on her sheet. Ratio scowled as usual, then returned to his test.

I retrieved my half a pencil from my pocket and wondered, with dizzying confusion, how the jacket I had nuked just a short while ago was back on my body, splattered with my blood and sweat.

With shaking hands, I looked at the first question on the test:

What have you learned about the Grands?

I hesitated, my stomach queasy, and then an electrical shock jolted through my body, hard enough to wrench my muscles and pull my bones out of place.

After that, with tears leaking down my face, I gripped my pencil and started writing. *Finish this test, Bel,* I told myself. *Or you'll die Here.*

Ep 36

He's Already Asleep

"Lie down and take a rest if you're so tired."

But I was already lying down. My face was squeezed into a cushioned hole, my body spread out on a padded table, belly down. Each of my limbs was pulled so taut that I thought they might snap at the joints.

I tried to ask what was happening, but there was no way I could. It was not a speaking day for me. The gag fit snug in my mouth, and I could not move my head to the left or right. My eyes were open, though, and I could see the feet of the Grades walking by, their shoes covered with white drawstring bags, the ivory tiles glistening.

"I'm fine. I can push through."

"Alright then, let's get going. Put him to sleep for this one," one of the Grades said, their words muffled by masks I couldn't see.

"He's already asleep," the other replied.

But I wasn't. I wasn't asleep. I could hear them speaking, see them walking. I felt the restraints on the table ripping my sternum apart, straining every muscle. I was so very awake.

I tried to speak up. To say anything. But the grunting noises I managed were not received by the Grades.

I closed my eyes and tried to cry. Bel cried when she was upset, when things made her afraid. And it seemed to help her. But the tears did not come. They were so beautiful when they rolled down her chin, dangling off the tip of her nose. No such beauty would grace me.

I thought about Helix. About Cacophony and Iris and how I even missed them. I missed stretching and walking with them while they glared at me. I missed the sneaky threats at night and the way it felt to have someone near me who understood where I came from, even if they resented where I was going.

I missed Hafiz and the worry he took on for my benefit. How he guarded me, even if it was to use me. Or rather, to prepare me to be used. But Bel said he was dead. It didn't seem possible, but she said it was true. He had always been There. *Why would Bel lie? She wouldn't. She wouldn't.*

"What are the adjustment specs?" the Grade asked.

"Taller. Just a hair."

"Hmm...we could adjust the soles of the feet? Add some lifts to the bone?"

"We would have to adjust his gait, then. Walking training again. It could take months. We don't have that kind of time."

"No. But the spine would take just as long to adjust. And the knees would take even longer. Skull would mess with his proportions, so that's not a real possibility."

"How about the neck?"

"Now that could work. Wouldn't affect his gait so much. Just some retraining on cranial positions. Minor adjustments. Painful, though."

"Yes, but speed over comfort right now. We have to remember what's at stake here."

"Time. But we cannot risk his perfection. No sloppy work."

"Yes." The voice of the Grade drifted off, as if he was pondering something. "How much longer do you think?"

"I can't say...."

"I know, but...what do you *think*?"

"I can't share those thoughts with you. I am not even supposed to be thinking them in the first place."

"But—"

"Enough."

The frazzled Grade got quiet. And then he spoke in a whisper, like someone was listening in on their conversation. "I am afraid. God Across knows I'm afraid."

"Of course you are. We all are. But we are making more progress than we could have ever hoped. Now is the time to press forward. To focus on the results. Time waits for no man, Cyrilus. Not me. Not you. Not even this Glimpse."

"You're right. You're always right."

"We get this taken care of, we can go home. Wouldn't you like that? I know I would like that more than anything."

"Yes. *Home*."

"Alright then." The sound of gloved hands giving a sharp clap. "Everyone ready? Sterilize the site. We have a cervical vertebra to elongate."

Ep 37

Good News

"Bellanueva, we have good news." Cyrilus smiled, but the dark circles around his eyes prevented him from looking any degree happier.

"I want to go home," I said as clearly as I could. I bounced my leg so fast I could have worn a hole in the dingy tiles. The places where the electrodes were attached to me still burned. I smelled cooking flesh and knew it was me. "That's all I want right now. To go *home*."

"Hear me out," the old man said, holding up a gloved hand.

"What was that test?" I asked. A sob squeezed out with my words. "What the hell on earth was that test?"

"Bel. You are very—"

"No, no, no. I want out. I want out of Here. And There. I want to go anywhere that's far away from you."

"Listen to me."

"No!"

"Bel—"

"No!"

I stood up and limped to the classroom door. Here Center couldn't hold me hostage forever. I shook the handle with all my strength, but the door wouldn't open. Like it had been bolted shut. I banged on it, sobbing, but no one heard. If they could hear me, no one cared.

"Bel, you're wasting time. Please. Sit down. Let me explain. Everything will feel much better if I explain."

I walked back over and did my best to kick over the chair and desk I'd been sitting on. I screamed at the old Grade. No words. Just noise. Finally, when I was too tired to see, I sank to to the floor in the middle of the empty classroom.

"Why did you ask me those kinds of questions?" I said. I spread myself out on the linoleum tiles so I could stare at the ceiling. I imagined a strange clock up there, counting down to zero. But really, there was only a broken ceiling fan and flickering overhead lights.

"The test questions progress as trainees move forward."

"I know how tests work, Cyrilus. Why were those the questions you asked? You're trying to make me into a crazy person. You're trying to—"

"We wanted to see what you notice."

"I notice nothing."

"You notice too much, Bellanueva."

The tears slid down my temples and into my hair. I tried to imagine Confía, with her curvy hips bumping mine as we washed dishes together. But all I felt was the brightness of the lights. Even my face was tired.

"What did you do to my sister?"

"Your sister is just as she was."

"Why? Why are you doing this to people? Let her go."

"We need her. We need you. We need you all to make Marrow as beautiful as possible."

I squeezed my eyes shut as tight as I could. "He doesn't deserve what you're trying to do to him."

"And exactly what are we trying to do to him, Bel?"

My inhale rattled. "Test question number 203: How does pain impact beauty? Number 204: How does fear impact beauty? Number 205: How does abandonment impact beauty? Number 206: How does friendship impact beauty? You guys are bastards. You're monsters. You can't do this to actual people. We're actual people. We're actual people. We're...actual people."

"We're running out of time, Bel."

"I don't know. What. That. Means."

"Good," Cyrilus sighed. "We need you to play along."

"You're insane."

"We need him to be beautiful."

"You're insane."

"If you ever want any of us to get home, you need to do this. You need to make him beautiful."

I sat up, gasping as sharp pains riddled my body. "I'm not going to hurt Marrow. I won't."

Cyrilus shook his head. "He'll be hurt no matter what you choose. We are asking you to give him a life. Can't you do that? Doesn't he deserve that?"

"You want me to lie to him. About you. About what the Grades are doing to the Glimpses. To the Grits. To the Grands. You want me to trick him into loving me...for you."

"Yes."

"I won't do it."

"Then you'll die. Do you understand? If you don't help us willingly, your life will be used for our purposes. He will lose you. He will be alone. And you, Bel, will be dead."

Ep 38

The Grades Had A Strange Way

The Grades gave me a room. This was probably the most disconcerting thing that had happened to me in all my days. Worse than the Grit presentation. Worse than Confía kicking me out of the house. Not because the room caused me any pain, but because there was no place to fit it into my brain.

The Grade room itself was small, like most Grit sleeping areas. A toilet in the corner. A small basin with running water. A mattress on the floor. But it was cleaner than most East West homes, the whole thing smelling of sanitation products and leverage. The scent of Grades. Sterilization with a slight whiff of Thereness.

Two other elements of my new accommodations made me want to take my skin off and get in an acid bath.

The first was the pictures on the walls. They were not in frames, like I'd seen people keep in their homes, though my family was not the sentimental sort and never bothered with things like that. Every four-hundred-day cycle, Here Center took one photo of any family who wanted one. Some put them in frames on their walls, but no one really understood why that was a thing to be done. The De Leons had never had our pictures taken. My mother said they made her sad, and my father didn't care about anything enough to put a frame around it. Secretly, I always thought it was because my parents had so many children with other people that they didn't know how to count them, much less assemble us all for a snapshot.

But the pictures on the walls of the Grade room were not of families and not in frames. They were plastered to the walls themselves. It was like I was living in the picture rather than looking at one from afar. There were people in the photos. They laughed and smiled, but it was clear to me that they couldn't actually have been related. It was like...fake families. Pretenders who didn't really know each other and who weren't really happy when they smiled. They ate at restaurants much fancier than the taco shop and snuggled in beds with clean white sheets on them. One group was sipping colorful drinks on top of an enormous ship in the middle of the biggest pond I'd ever seen.

These picture walls made me feel trapped, like I was living in the same nightmare as the people in the photos—forced to smile and to wrap an arm around a stranger.

The second unbearable feature of my new room was the small clock. Half its face was blank, and the other half held numbers counting down to zero. It ticked so loudly that I had to cover my ears to just hear myself panic.

I tried to pull it off the wall, but it was mounted securely, and I only succeeded in damaging my fingertips.

"Is the room to your liking?" Cyrilus said, appearing behind me and scaring me three quarters to death.

"How did you get in here?" I asked him, still trying to wrench the clock off the wall. "I locked the door behind me when I walked in."

He didn't seem surprised by my efforts to remove the time piece. He ignored it altogether. "The locks only work when we need them to."

I blinked. "That is the creepiest thing you've said to me yet."

He dismissed my comment. "Will you be comfortable here?"

"No. But I've never been comfortable a day in my life. That, and I don't want to be doing this at all. But nothing I want seems to matter. Doesn't make sense to start complaining now."

Cyrilus nodded. "Well said." He motioned to the curtained closet in the corner of my room. "New clothes for you. And we will need you to begin assessing in the next thirty minutes. Will you be ready?"

"I was hoping I could lie down. You know...since you had some guy punch me in the face so many times?"

"Alright then. An hour."

"Tomorrow."

He scoffed. "That's too much time wasted."

"Listen, hombre. I'm going to clean myself up. I'm going to eat whatever food you've provided for me. I'm going to lie down and sleep. And then—not a minute sooner—I will begin assessing. These aren't terms, Cyrilus. It's what I am humanly capable of at this moment in time. Do you understand what I am saying to you?"

He sighed. "An extra long assessment tomorrow, then. And I will need you to begin teaching as well."

"Teaching? Teaching who? Teaching what?"

"Your methods. But we will discuss this tomorrow. Enjoy your rest, Bellanueva. And congratulations on your new position. The Grades officially welcome you."

He left, closing the door behind him. *Good. Now to find Marrow and run like hell.* But when I twisted the handle, the door wouldn't yield. *Locked. From the outside.*

The Grades had a strange way of welcoming people.

Ep 39

Or I Do

They sat me up in a chair. The strap across my forehead kept me pressed to the headrest. It immobilized me until my neck could properly heal. It was strange, being taller even by the tiniest fraction of a length. The world was shaped differently. All the vantages changed. Things that once looked big seemed rather small.

Bel did not seem smaller, though, when she walked into the room. She wore the same kind of clothes she always had. A shirt with holes and snags in it, beaten shoes, and shorts. Her face was still healing—bruised and burnt—but clean. Her hair was loose around her shoulders. I knew she would pull it up on top of her head once she got to thinking. I would get to see the way her hands moved, the skin of her scarred knuckles shifting as she twisted the brown waves into place.

A Grade handed her a clipboard, and she tossed it across the room without a thought. It clattered into equipment I could not see, as doing so would have required me to turn my head.

It was not a turning day for me.

"Get out," she told the Grade, tossing her head toward the door.

The Grade hesitated, eyeing the discarded clipboard, I assumed. Or perhaps it was the damaged equipment they didn't prefer.

Bel raised her voice, her words clipping. "Either you get out, or I do."

The Grade audibly sighed and left, shoulders tensed beneath the bulky white suit.

Bel did indeed pull her hair up, her brown eyes on me. Then she walked over and put her hand on mine. Her thumb rubbed the veins on my wrist. It made me take a breath.

After she studied me for far too long, she spoke. "I'll make them give you meds. The pain is too much."

"It's alright," I said. Speaking was uncomfortable. My voice pushed against my delicate spine, causing prickles of sharp pain.

"It's *not* alright," she said. She was angry. I had seen anger before. Iris got angry sometimes. It was part of her beauty. And there was no mistaking. Bel was also beautiful when she was angry, her eyebrows creased and her eyes focused on the problem with pure intensity. "None of this is alright. I'm not going to just let them hurt you. I don't care what the Grands need. I don't care about any of those people."

She started to pull away, but I gripped her hand as best I could, my fingers clutching her wrist. The movement made me whimper, and I hated the look that crossed her face when I did. "Don't go yet," I said. "Stay with me. Ask me questions."

She leaned closer. "Marrow, I can't ask you questions when you can hardly speak. When you're hurt. I'm not going to hurt you like they do."

"Bel...ask the questions." I swallowed and had to close my eyes. When I opened them, Bel had tears in hers. "If you ask...they will let you keep seeing me."

She wiped at her nose. "Fine." She crossed the room to retrieve her clipboard and glanced at it. "They want me to ask you about how you felt when the Grades watched you."

I thought back to their strange faces, how they stared without reacting to what they saw. "They made me feel like...I wasn't real. Like maybe they couldn't see me."

She shook her head, setting the clipboard down again. "Marrow, they gave me a room. They're treating me like I'm one of them. But on that test, they asked me questions about my mother, about Lǎobǎn. About you and Hafiz. About Mango and Ratio. They know everything about us. Marrow, they asked me about the *tacos*." She squeezed her eyes shut. "How do they know all this? Did you tell them?"

"I don't...even know what some of those things are, Bel. What's a mango ratio?"

She groaned into her hands. "How are they watching us so closely? How?"

"I don't think they are *watching*, Bel."

"Then how did they know exactly which questions to ask?"

"Maybe...we're predictable."

She sat up straight, her eyes wide as she gasped. "Marrow," she said. "You beautiful angel." Then she took the clipboard, flipping over the paper stuck to it and lifting the pen. "Let's get started."

Ep 40

That You Were Wonderful

My pencil scratched with fury across the paper. I knew I would run out of time to share the hatchling of a plan with Marrow, so I went as fast as possible, my brain flaring to life. It helped to imagine electrodes stuck to my temples and chest, sending shockwaves of excruciating pain through my body as I worked. Nothing motivated me like excruciation.

"Bel, you look like you are in great distress," Marrow said from his chair, his head strapped to it. I could feel his eyes following my movements. "Why are you doing this?"

"Callate. I'm thinking."

I separated the paper into segments. One section would be for the Grits. One for the Grands. And in the middle, overlapping both sections, the Grades. *Grits are to remain Here and keep to themselves.*

Grands remain There and do the same. But Grades...Grades are both Here and There. Technically working with both groups.

When I read the questions on the last test I'd been given, I was convinced the Grades were watching us. *But what if they're not watching? What if they're predicting? And using us to test those predictions?*

"The only way to know for sure is to make our own predictions," I said out loud.

"What?"

I was startled because I hadn't realized I'd spoken audibly and that Marrow could hear me. "Oh. We have to conduct our own studies. On the *Grades*. Then we'll know what they're trying to do. And most importantly...why. If we know why, we can concoct an escape plan. And then you and I can get out of here, Marrow. Get away from this."

"But...I don't know how to predict," he said.
He sounded tired. It made me want to rip the building apart.

"Yes you do. You predict all the time. You're very good at it. You predicted that you could walk from There to Here. And you predicted where I might live when you found my house. And you predicted that guava nectar would taste good, or you wouldn't have taken your first sip."

"I didn't predict anything about the drink. I only predicted that you were wonderful. If you said it was good, I knew it would be."

My cheeks warming embarrassed me profoundly. I cleared my throat. "Yes. Thank you."

"It wasn't a compliment. I was simply stating predictions."

I couldn't help chuckling. "You think you're funny, huh?"

He smiled. "I predicted you would think so."

I pointed my pencil at him. "Very nice, 'Row."

"But...what sort of predictions do we need to test?"

I referred to the results of my crazed note-taking. "We use their methods on them. Two days of being completely normal. One day of being completely unpredictable. Make every third day's choices as different from your usual as possible. But keep repeating that third day until you notice a pattern shift in their behavior to match yours."

"So if usually I wake up and stretch right away, do that on days one and two. But on every day three, throw my cot across the room instead?"

"Exactly. And—this is the most important part—pay attention to how the Grades adjust. My guess is that they will alter their predictions and begin to anticipate your random third-day choices."

"This is how we will know they are indeed predicting us?"

I nodded. Since I could hear a Grade coming to end my session with Marrow, I hurried over and kissed his cheek. I meant it to be a quick peck, but I ended up lingering. His skin was so impossibly smooth that for a moment, I was afraid I'd hurt him.

But, his head trapped in place, he smiled at me, his dark eyes shimmering.

"What was *that*?" he asked.

"It's called a kiss."

"It is different than a hug. Why was it so...different?"

"It means...something else." How was I going to explain this to someone as important as Marrow?

"What does it mean?"

"Hugs are for comfort. Kisses are for...."

"Pleasure?"

"Uh...yes. Well said."

"It was *very* pleasing. Your lips are even softer than I predicted."

I blinked, shocked as I straightened up. "You...think about my lips?"

"I think about every part of you."

But before I could tell him that sometimes I cried in the dark at night because I would never be able to fall asleep beside him, the Grade walked in and ushered me out of the room.

Ep 41

Third Day Of The Third Week

The third day. I had been waiting for it all week. It seemed like I was always waiting for the third day to come around once more. Each time, I listened to everything Bel told me. I followed all her rules and guidelines. Every morning, I made the same movements. I rose and stretched, as always. Feeding tube placements. I was weighed, measured, temperature taken. They evaluated my mental well-being with three questions. I gave the same answers I always did. Then on to the rest of my day, which included milk baths, mud burials, and scheduled rests. Those were the more pleasant parts.

In the afternoons, they sometimes let me talk to Bel.

But finally—at last—it was the morning of the third day. And every third day was my favorite. And

I had never been so excited to realize I was opening my eyes. *Here we go.*

I got off my cot and crawled underneath it, same as I did on the other third days. Lying on my back, I pressed my bare feet against the springs above me. And then, after a few breaths, I kicked with all my strength, and the lightweight cot went careening across the room. It clattered against the wall, leaving a decent dent in the smooth surface.

I laughed. That surprised me more than my willingness to destroy my sleeping paraphernalia, particularly because I had not laughed any other time I performed this trick. I was all alone, with no Bel to create humor for me, and still I laughed. The sound coming from within me was lovely but scary. Perhaps the very scariness of it—the way it rose and fell without being controlled or measured—is what made it beautiful to me.

It was strange not to stretch when I stood up. My muscles remained tight, and my bones creaked with each movement I made. But I enjoyed the uncomfortable sensation because it was caused by me and not by Grades in white or Glimpses in jealous fits.

The Grades came in as they always did, and they meant to escort me to get my bloodwork and feeding tube arranged. But every time they put the long, transparent cord into my feeding tube, I pulled it back out. I repeated this four or five times, until the sensitive abdominal skin around my feeding tube was raw from the aggravation.

Finally, the Grade, realizing that my beauty was being reduced, gave up on feeding me altogether. I was surprised they did not try to bind my hands as they usually did during my third-day resistances. *It is working.* I had never been so delighted to go hungry. The feeling reminded me of meeting Bel at her house that night and of the deep ache in my stomach, just beneath my heart, that let me know I was alive.

I stood to my feet, leaving my examination chair behind as the Grades whispered to one another, scribbling on clipboards with frantic pencils.

"I want something!"

The cluster of Grades turned white-clad heads to me in unison.

"You heard me," I shouted to them. "I, Marrow, want something!" Now, I was not supposed to be shouting this. It wasn't part of my scheduled un-scheduling. I wasn't sure what was overtaking me, but it overtook.

The Grades also did not know what was happening. Maybe other Glimpses had the programming to say such things, to possess and express such bold desires. I was supposed to be self-fulfilled. Self-contained. Calm and slow moving. Sourced from the very center of earth. Rich and whole and holy. A living tectonic plate. I was not supposed to throw tantrums and make demands.

"Bring me my shirt!" I said. "And bring me tacos! Tacos! Tacos! This is what I want!"

Slowly, one of the Grades—obviously in shock—began to write something down on their clipboard.

"I want tacos! And juice that comes from fruit! And...and something *new*! Something I've never tried before!" I had no idea how to express the feeling pulsing in my chest. It overtook me. It overtook me. So I snatched a clipboard from an unsuspecting Grade. "I want something! I want something! Bring me food! And...." I snapped the clipboard in half over my knee and threw the pieces in different directions. "I want Bel."

Ep 42

And I Lost Count

I waited and waited for the Grades to bring my Bel to me. It seemed to take days. And I lost count of whether I was on day one or two or three. I started to wonder whether there were ever such things as day fours or fives, and just how many days there once used to be. There was only ever day three or not day three for me. *Are the Grades counting? Have they predicted my unpredictability yet?* I wished I could ask Hafiz if he noticed. But I could not. He never came to visit anymore. *What could be so interesting in his room? What was so much dearer to him than me?*

Finally. I sensed her coming down the hall. Not because I had some special skill, but because the Grades minding my wellbeing began to adjust themselves. She was coming. They prepared. *Good,* I thought. *Bel deserves to be prepared for.*

The door opened. It was her. It was her.

Her brown eyes held the same question they always did when she saw me. When we first met, I didn't know what the question was. But the longer I knew her, the clearer her unspoken language became. She always wanted to know one thing. *Are you alright?*

I was hungry and worried about the counting—the worrying, of course, would upset Hafiz—but otherwise elated. And yes, I had been losing count, but it was worth it to keep trying. Day one, day two, day three.

She looked around the room in silence. I hadn't thought how the wrecked lab room might make it seem like I was in some sort of distress. She turned those eyes back on me. "Marrow...*Dios*." Her voice was thick, like she needed to swallow.

"Everything is alright," I said to her. The Grade escorting her gripped her upper arm tight in his hands, ensuring she did not have the freedom to walk around the room.

"Marrow...you can't be...serious..." she said. She placed her words so carefully. Bel was always so careful.

I smiled. A thousand gol down the drain. "Something wonderful happened. And all the feelings were too strong to keep inside me."

She squirmed, obviously wishing her arm was free but knowing the Grade wouldn't loosen his gloved grip. She seemed different than when we'd met, back then with her skinned knee and her bouncing hair. If I was hungry, Bel was tired. "What sort of feelings, mi amor? Bad ones?"

I closed my eyes as I remembered the feelings in question. My body became warm, my head light. It was like dreaming while awake. "They were very good. I...laughed when I felt them."

Her mouth twitched, but she glanced at the Grade with caution, her eyes darkening. "You had fun, huh?"

Fun. Cacophony loved having fun. He would giggle and giggle, standing on his hands and moving about the room, then rolling on the floor until he was dizzy. I always thought he was demented. But maybe there was more to it. Maybe I was too simple to understand. Simple, beautiful Marrow.

"I think so. Fun...." I cleared my mind and refocused on Bel. "And then I decided I wanted to see you. Isn't that strange, Bel?"

"Fun is better shared," she explained. "It increases the feelings."

I wanted to move toward her. Because I wanted to hold her hand. And I wanted to make her look less afraid. I wanted to put my lips to her cheek like she'd put hers to mine, and for her to think my lips were softer than she expected. But I could not move toward her.

It was no longer a moving day for me.

Ep 43

Third Days And One-Sided Conversations

"I cannot do this. Please. Please."

My inhales trembled, and there were no exhales left. I was on my knees in the room the Grades had given me. Cyrilus stood at my door, his liver-spotted face drawn into an uncomfortable stare. I was acutely aware that he took note of the tears that splattered on the floor but that he did not care about any of them. He did, however, clinically assess each one. How fast were they falling? Soon, they would pin me down as well and take samples. How salty? How much volume?

"Bellanueva, you must learn to control yourself if you are to remain in this program."

"I don't want to remain in this program! Aren't you hearing the words I am saying to you? Escúchame!

I cannot do this. It is not bearable. I want to go home."

"That is no longer a possibility for you. Not in the way you think."

"What do you *mean*? Where is my family?"

"Bel—"

"Then have me removed! I would rather that than put Marrow through this. *I cannot do it*. This is worse than torture. This is worse than dying."

"I understand what you are feeling—"

"No! You don't! He trusts me. Marrow...he adores me. And he is not some experiment, he is a person. A living, breathing, feeling person with hopes and fears, dreams and nightmares. There is no justification for this."

"There is only justification for this. This is the justification."

"I won't do another sequence. I won't. You...you"—I gasped. That was when I realized I would pass out. I wished I would die, but no. People like me didn't get off so easy in life. People like me suffered. That was justification. "You are literally tearing him apart."

"It is a reconstruction. We are making him more whole. These things are a matter of perspective."

"Why? *Why* are you doing it?"

"Knowing why something is done does not change the fact that it must be done, Bellanueva. You must be tested, and Marrow must be beautiful."

"And you? You must abdicate?"

"I," he nodded his head with a sigh, "must grade."

"No." I slammed my fist into the floor so hard that my knuckles cracked. "I won't let you. I'm going to stop you. *All of you*."

"Alright," Cyrilus said, a hint of sorrow in his voice. And a bit of relief. "If you must." And he left my room, the lock clicking in place behind him.

I sprang up and ran at the door, twisting the handle and pounding. But it would not open.

"I won't do it!" I screamed through the walls. The pictures on my walls were changed every third day, matching the pattern. A fake family riding horses and laughing in the sunshine, all wearing perfect, colorful clothing. Their teeth gleamed white, but their eyes were all afraid. Or some children playing with an elaborate plastic toy. The picture was taken mid-laugh, except I could tell that the children weren't really friends and weren't really laughing.

These pictures haunted me. I could not sleep at night with their frightened eyes staring at me, their anxious smiles looming over my bed. I'd tried to scrape their faces off the walls, but I'd only succeeded at ripping bits of my fingernails from their beds.

"I won't do it!"

I ran to my closet and ripped the clothes from where they'd been hung. Every hole-ridden shirt, every pair of worn jeans. All the tattered sneakers. Clothes I'd never even seen before. New every cycle, yet perfectly used. All in my size. All with the odor of Dime Block ground into the threading.

I tore at the fabric but I couldn't rip it. *Am I this weak? Or is it made of something unbreakable? Something invincible*? The words 'Grit presentation' crept up the base of my spine like an electric shock.

"I will stop you," I sobbed, even though I knew they weren't listening. "I must stop you."

And when I curled into myself, lying on the floor and pressing the clothes to my face—because in my heart, no matter how far away I'd tried to get, I knew I loved the smell of Dime Block, of home, of familia—I remembered the hastily scratched words of my mother's note. *You're not wrong, Bel.*

I whispered this to myself, to Marrow, wherever he was—anywhere except with me—until I fell into shallow sleep for the night.

Ep 44

Reinforcements

"Bel? Bel!"

The whisper outside my door brought me out of a fitful sleep. I sat up on the floor in the dark, wondering if I was hearing ghosts.

"Dios? Is that you?" I answered. I had no idea why, but my mom always taught me that if I ever heard something strange calling my name in the dead of night, it had better be God.

"What? No. It's us, Bel. Open the door."

I inched closer to the door, leaving my assigned Grit clothing on the floor in a crumpled pile. "Who is 'us'?"

"Mango," the soft voice said. "And Ratio. Can you let us in?"

"You're here?! I thought I was alone in this place. I thought I was the only one." Heart pumping, I jiggled the handle, even though I knew for certain the door wouldn't budge. "It's locked. But can't you open it from the outside? Cyrilus comes in whenever he wants."

"No," Mango said. "It's some sort of time-activated lock. Ratio hacked ours but yours is tricky. We thought maybe you'd locked it from the inside."

"No. I can't get out. Wait, do they lock you guys in your rooms too?"

"Most of the time." There was a pause. "Ratio is working on it. Stand back."

I waited and waited and realized all at once how desperately I wished I had anyone to talk to. Someone I could look at who didn't think of me as part of some elaborate project. When the lock clicked and the door swung open, I scurried backward, making room for my friends to hurry inside.

To my surprise, Mango crawled into my room on all fours and threw her arms around me, squeezing tight. "I thought you were dead," she whispered.

I squeezed back. "Are some of the other trainees... did they kill them?"

Ratio also crawled in, pulling the door shut behind him. "The others were removed, we think. But maybe not. No way to know for sure. We thought *you* were removed until we heard Cyrilus mention your name to another Grade. We all got partnered off and then disappeared, couple by couple. Do you not have a partner?"

"No, no partner. It's just me." Thankfully Ratio and I didn't hug. But I was still happy to see him, even with his habit of being maximum irksome in the past. He'd still come through for me somehow when I needed help.

"What do they make you do every day, Bel?" Mango asked. "We take tests. All. Day. Long."

Ratio nodded. "Sometimes I design tests for Mango. Sometimes she designs for me. Sometimes we take tests designed by the Grades. Over and over. And over. And over."

Mango rubbed his arm gently, trying to soothe him out of his loop. He swallowed, but I imagined in his brain he was still stuck, still repeating...over and over.

Mango held up her hands to reveal white bandages on all her fingertips. "My fingers bleed. From holding the pencil. Sometimes they give us glue to help us hold on for longer. And I have sores where they hook up the electrodes. We test for so long, I lose track of time. I don't know if I should be tired or energetic, if it's morning or night."

"There is no time in this place, Mango," Ratio said. It was difficult to make them out in the shadows, and the lights being on or off was out of my control. But I could see just enough to observe their features. And I heard a crack in his voice that told me he was not alright. "I didn't even get to tell my family I was leaving. They probably think I'm dead."

Luckily, my family would not be looking for me. I pushed that bit of pain further down in my chest, aware that it would bubble up again at an even less convenient time. "How did you break into the doors?" I asked, hoping to distract him but also eager to learn how I could find Marrow and escape.

"I fixed up lots of cars back on Dime Block. And most of my Grade tests include some kind of mechanics, so it's fair to say I know my way around electrical systems. I basically just short the timers on the doors. They reboot after that, and so far, the Grades can't tell we've been tampering with them. Yours was double secure though. Like...another locking mechanism activated once the first failed. But with the correct synchronization, I got them both shorted at just the right time."

"You use some sort of device?"

"I know what you're thinking, Bel. We can't use the devices to get out of here, or I would be gone already. The door to get out of this place is like nothing I've ever seen. No offense, but I would have left you both here in a heartbeat if it meant I could escape this nightmare."

"If I—*when* I leave—I have to be careful. Lăobăn will be looking for me. I've made such a mess of things in East West, I probably wouldn't even make it to Dime Block alive. I don't blame you for wanting to keep your distance from the catastrophe that is my life, Ratio. Lăobăn is no joke."

"Who?" Ratio and Mango said in unison, their brows furrowed in matching confusion.

"Very funny, Horatio." *Mango might not know the notorious Lăobăn, but Ratio knew him well enough to warn me not to go home that night he was outside my house murdering my father and driving his fists into my sister.* "Lăobăn. The Lăobăn."

"I don't know who you mean, Bel." Ratio said. And it looked like he meant it.

Ep 45

Things To Know For Sure

I would either cry or throw up if I tried to understand what was happening in my life. But then, I took a deep breath and thought through things. I did this for some time, with Ratio and Mango sitting and watching me while I said nothing, only staring down at my lap. In this position, I reviewed all the facts that I could, recalling every incident in my recent memories. I skipped all the ones with Marrow in them, because he was different and special, and I reviewed those in my private moments, when I could admit to myself how much he made my heart ache.

Finally, I had it sorted. I looked at my friends. Fellow trainees. Whatever they were. "No. You're lying." I balled my hands into fists and realized crying was never a non-option. I fought the tears though. No time to cry. No time to be hurt or offended. I had done that all night long, sleeping on the floor in my awful room. And I would do it later, when I was alone once again. Now it was time to speak. "You know exactly who Lǎobǎn is. And the doors aren't time locked. Someone let you in here. You didn't think I was removed." My breath rattled. "You've been watching me. You've been studying me. You came here to talk to me as some sort of plan. An experiment."

"No, Bel, we—"

"I won't believe anything else, so you can drop it. They make me do the same thing to Marrow. They make me lie to him. Make me pretend. But it goes layers and layers deep. You are lying to me while I lie to Marrow." I scooted away from them. I needed some distance. Some distance from the relief I almost had, from the surge of hope that wracked my body when I thought I didn't have to be alone. "Are you doing it willingly? Are they...forcing you?"

Mango and Ratio glanced at each other. It was fleeting. But I knew what it meant. Me figuring out what they were doing was off script. And they didn't know the best way to answer my question.

"I was never going to be a Grade, was I? I was invited to the group under false pretenses." It all unfolded. The whole thing. All the lies falling like curtains. "I never got a perfect score on my test. I never made it to training on my own merit."

I pointed at Ratio. "That's why I'd never seen you in Dime Block before. You don't live there. You were planted. You were *lying*."

I looked to Mango. "You befriended me on purpose. To guide me. To influence me. To monitor me. To study me. You never gave any actual shits about me. Not ever."

I shook my head, my breath starting to pick up, my fingers going cold. "Tell me the truth. About everything."

"Bel...you're jumping to a lot of conclusions," Mango said. "You need to stay calm."

"My sister? My dad? My mom?" I visualized my childhood home, the junky yard with the old broken-down cars. The room where Confía entertained Lǎobǎn's clients. The toddlers screaming and clawing at my calves to be picked up and held and fed. "Where did all those children at our house even come from?" I ran my hands into my hair so I could feel my scalp under my fingernails. "Is Confía actually my sister? Where are my older brothers? Where did they go? Were they real?

Any of them?" I was no longer exhaling. "I want to see my mom."

Ratio put a hand out as if it would calm me, but no amount of well wishes and gentle touches would distract me this time. "I want to see my mom. They told me she was dead, but she's not, is she? Where did she go? Do you have her?"

Mango looked worried, her lips tightening, her brown skin wrinkling along her forehead. "Bellanueva, you need to calm down. You have this all wrong."

I laughed at her. I laughed at all of them. I spent so much time feeling sorry for Marrow. Believing he was the one being observed, being manipulated, being adjusted. But he was not the only one at all. "I'm not wrong, Mango. I'm not wrong. That's about the only thing I know for sure."

Ep 46

The Sound Of A Snap

"Take me to my mom."

"We have no idea where your mom would be," Ratio said, shaking his head. "I thought you said she was dead."

"She's not dead."

"Well, that's great then, Bel, but I don't know where she is."

I stood up calmly while they remained sitting on my floor, stepped forward, and rammed my knee into Horatio's nose harder than I ever thought I could. I jumped on him, grappling him with my knees around his neck, and squeezed. He scratched at me, his arms flailing wildly, but I wouldn't let go.

Mango inhaled, preparing to scream, but I looked her in the eye with what I guessed was an expression of complete insanity.

"Keep quiet, and I let him live. Scream, and I'll kill you too."

She flopped her mouth closed, her brown eyes opened wide and her coiled locks shaking around her head. "I'll stop you," she said, speaking just above a whisper.

"You can't directly influence me, can you? Can't force me. You're supposed to suggest and observe. Aren't you, Mango? Aren't you?"

Her eyes filled with tears as she nodded her head. "Please don't kill him."

"Are they watching?"

She nodded again. "Bel, let him go."

But I didn't. I didn't. I held tighter and tighter until he stopped moving altogether. And then I held on for longer. Finally, I let go, uncurling my limbs and straightening my back as I stood. Maybe Ratio was dead. Maybe he was unconscious. But I didn't have the desire to check.

"Get up," I told Mango. "Now."

She hurried off the ground, sniffling to keep her nose from leaking all over her shirt. "You... killed him?"

"You're next," I said. And I was so surprised that I meant it. My heart hadn't beat so steady in a long time. "Unless you tell me the truth."

She nodded, her eyes darting to Ratio's still form, then to me, then back again.

"What is the clock?"

"The...the clock?"

"The big clock on the ceiling of Grand Tower. The clock where Marrow lives. What is it?"

Mango shook her head. "I don't know what you're talking about. I promise I don't know."

"Where is my mom?"

She cowered as if I were going to hit her, though I hadn't moved. "Bel, I don't know anything about your mother. I swear."

I forced down the flutter of despair in my chest. "Is my mom my mom? Is my sister my sister?"

"I...think...."

"God Across, Mango! What *do* you know?" I lowered my head and pulled at my hair as hard as I could, hoping it would center me somehow. "Do you know where Marrow is?"

"Yes."

"Yes?" I looked up at her, releasing my poor hair. "Take me to him. Now."

She started to shake her head but I ran at her, swinging my fists. "Take me! Now! Take me to him!"

She shrieked and then pulled away from me. "Alright, Bellanueva, yes!"

I realized I had left long welts on her face and forearms. But I told myself that I didn't care. That whatever this test was needed to be over, or I would die. I would die.

So I followed Mango a few steps forward until we arrived at the room directly across the corridor from mine. He had been right beside me the whole time. *The whole goddamn time.* This whole place was a figment of unprocessable terror. I felt my breathing grow rapid, my hands start to sweat once more. Who could fabricate lies so intricate that they became someone's reality? That they became comforting? That they became home? *And for the love of God Across, why would they do such a thing?*

"Here," Mango said with one long sniffle, pointing at the door that stood identical to mine. "Here. Are you happy?"

"No. I'm not *happy*, Mango. Open the door."

Ep 47

Already Filled My Pockets

Mango put her hand to the door, and green lights beamed beneath her palm. I had never seen anyone open the door like this, but my brain had already been coated in a thick layer of deception, so it didn't surprise me. I pulled the door open.

"What about Ratio?" Mango cried. "We can't just leave him there. He could be alive. He could be *dead*."

Ratio wasn't dying. He was dead. I shoved Mango into the room ahead of me. "Sit in the corner and don't say anything unless I ask you a direct question, or I swear to God Across, you will end up just like your boyfriend."

I surveyed the room. No Grades present, but beeping machines and other unnamed devices crowded the space. Marrow was lying on a cot, his eyes closed, and I tripped over many cords as I hurried to him.

"Marrow! Marrow, wake up." I touched his soft cheeks and exhaled with relief at how warm and alive he felt.

His eyelids fluttered open, and he smiled when he realized it was me. "Bel?" He sat up on his elbows. "I thought I was dreaming when I heard your voice."

"No, not dreaming. I'm really here." *Right? I'm really here.* "Now, are you hurt? We have to hurry."

He frowned, sitting up all the way on his cot. "We do?"

"Yes. I mean, if you want to come with me, then yes, we have to hurry—"

"You can't *leave*!" Mango shouted from the corner, her voice cracking with panic.

I grabbed the nearest piece of equipment I could find and hurled it at her so hard that it fractured into a million pieces when she ducked and it hit the wall. "Shut up, Mango, shut up!"

Marrow held my face in his hands, turning me to him so I could look into his eyes. "Breathe, Bel. Slow down."

I shook my head, plopping down beside him. "No, no. No breathing. No slowing down. This place is...it's not *real*. It's...I don't know what it is, Marrow, but I can't stay here and I also can't leave you here without you, so if you don't want to come with me, I don't know what I'm going to do—"

Marrow put his lips on mine and then grinned. "I did that."

I grinned back at him, even though most of my emotional signals still indicated that I desperately needed to throw up. "You did. It was good."

He nodded. "Let's go."

Just like that? Let's go? I was too stunned to say anything or even to process what was happening as he threw off his blanket and got out of his cot. He held out his hand to me, and when I hesitated, he took it anyway and pulled me to my feet. "How do we get out, Bel?"

I blinked myself back to focus. Then pointed at Mango. "That one will tell us."

She had curled herself into a ball on the floor, her forehead on her knees so we could not see her face.

"Mango, you're going to give us very clear instructions on how to get out of this place."

"I can't! I don't know how."

"Figure it out, Mango!" I screamed.

She crawled toward the door, but I grabbed her by the back of the shirt and dragged her the rest of the way. "If you won't tell me how to leave, then you're coming too."

A deep voice croaked. "What are you *doing*, Bellanueva?"

Cyrilus stood in the threshold of the door in his fresh lab coat, a frown on his wrinkled face.

I pointed a shaky finger at him. "Show us the way out."

"The way out? The way out of what?"

"Out! The...the way out...."

What did *I mean by out? Out of where? Of the room? Of the building? Out of this false reality?* I shook my head. I needed to focus. *Now is not the time to doubt yourself, Bel. You're not wrong. You're not.* "If you don't tell us how to get out, I'll...."

"You'll what? Haven't you done enough damage here? You have nearly ruined a Glimpse, who we desperately need, and you have murdered three of your colleagues—"

"Three?! I did not kill three people!"

"Horatio lies dead in the next room. And of course, Hafiz is gone. And Mervil."

"Mervil? How was he anything close to being my colleague?"

Cyrilus clamped his mouth shut as if he had misspoken.

"I don't care," I decided. "I don't care what sort of twisted, maniacal operation you're running, but Marrow and I are leaving. And if you don't show us how, I'll kill you too."

"You would not dare to—"

Mango screamed and kept screaming as blood poured from the old man's forehead. He fell like a downed electrical pole, careening into medical equipment as he went.

I turned to face Marrow, who stood in perfect elegance and grace behind me. "Marrow?"

"Yes?"

"Did you just...hurl a scalpel...into that Grade's head?"

"No."

I continued to stare. Mango continued to scream. "No? Porque...it sure seems like you did."

"It wasn't a scalpel. It was a drill bit. They are weighted better for throwing."

He sighed, his usually erect shoulders drooping. "I did another murder."

"Mmhmm."

"Do you still...want me to come with you?"

I laughed. A nice good belly laugh. The kind that made my toes curl. Finally, when I pulled myself together, I wiped the tears from my eyes. "Yeah, let's go. We'll figure it out. But probably best to grab some sharp objects. We might need to do a couple more murders in order to get out of here, 'Row."

Completely shirtless and with eyes like an angel's, he beamed at me. "I have already filled my pockets. Ready when you are."

Ep 48

The Ladder Episode

"This way," Marrow said. "To the roof. That's how I got out to come find you that first time, Bel."

We hurried through the hallways together, me in front and Marrow behind. I hoped no one would confront us. I didn't necessarily enjoy seeing scalpels sticking out of skulls. Things like that made my stomach hurt. But on the other hand, my stomach had been in constant clenched pain for as long as I could remember.

We climbed a set of metal stairs and opened one more door, and then we were on the roof. It was morning, which I didn't expect. The sorts of things we'd done made it seem like night would always linger. Like we would live the rest of our lives swimming through shadows. But no. The

sun gleamed in the blue sky like everything was alright in the world.

"Set her down and take a breath," I told Marrow.

"I don't really need a break," he countered. To be fair, he balanced Mango on his shoulder like she was no more than ten units. "Do you think *she* needs a break?"

Mango squirmed, screaming into her mouth gag. I poked at her fleshy hands and legs. "Seems like her circulation's fine. And her general level of pissed off is a good sign that she's doing alright, I'd say. We keep going."

Marrow nodded. "There's a ladder right over there. We can get down to the street and find a car." But when we approached the ladder, he hesitated.

"What's wrong?" I asked him. "You need a break after all?" He must have just been healed from a surgery. Who knows what adjustments he'd endured most recently. There was no way Marrow wasn't in pain.

"No," he said. "I'm fine. I was just thinking... about the other Glimpses. I feel guilty leaving them behind."

"Marrow...you weren't the one who left them behind. They left *you* behind. They disappeared.

Not one of them has come to check on you, look for you. In fact, maybe they went to wherever it is we're headed now. Maybe you'll see them again once we get there."

He sighed and nodded. "You're right, Bel. I don't even know where they are. And if they're at home, we'd only be captured trying to find them."

"If they are here, we can make a plan and come back for them, 'Row. We're not abandoning them. We're strategizing."

But we weren't doing that either. We were surviving.

"How do we get her down?" Marrow asked, pausing yet again at the top of the ladder. "I don't think I'm coordinated enough to descend the ladder while holding her."

Mango shrieked an objection. Apparently she wasn't much a fan of falling to her death either.

"Why don't you go down first, 'Row, and I'll toss her down to you. You've played catch before right?"

He stared at me. "I don't know what you mean."

"Playing catch?"

"What's 'playing'?"

A laugh burst from me. "It's similar to having fun."

He grinned. "Oh, I like that! Fun is...fun."

I matched his grin, and we stood there for a while like idiots, smiling at each other, before I snapped out of it. "Okay, well let's give it a try. That's the best any of us can do. Try." I bit my lip when the words left my mouth. "My mom used to say that."

"But now she's dead," Marrow said, sadness radiating from his beautiful face.

"Yeah. Now she's dead."

Marrow set Mango on the ground and made it down the ladder faster than I thought he would and looked at me, shielding his eyes. "Alright! Throw her down. Time for the fun!"

I dragged my former colleague to the edge of the building despite her writhing in an attempt to escape. "Don't worry," I said to her, "he's not going to drop you. Confía en mí." I translated for her, just in case. "Trust me." I don't know why I lied to the poor thing like that, but it made me feel better. I had no idea whether Marrow was capable of catching a hundred and thirty units of Grit-turned-Grade as she hurtled toward him. Nonetheless, I counted to tres and rolled her over the edge.

As she fell through the air, I realized with horror that perhaps Marrow did not know that counting

to three was a thing we did to prepare someone for what was coming. Perhaps the counting even distracted him, and he was standing there wondering why I had yelled out numbers. I waited to hear a splat, but instead heard the sound of straining.

When I peeked over the edge, Marrow was on his ass, a stunned Mango in his lap. "Got her!" He glowed up at me.

"Amazing!" And then I added, "Was it fun?"

"Well…it hurt more than I thought it would, and I got a bit nervous. So no, not that fun. I do not recommend."

I laughed as I climbed down the ladder. And we found a nice car with ease because people There did not bother locking their things away. With Mango in the back seat and no regard for traffic flow, we bolted away from the clock tower, from the adjustments and the lies, from the room with the pictures of people on the walls. From the Grade with the scalpel in his skull and the Glimpses we hadn't taken the time to locate.

I drove, and Marrow let his hand float on the wind outside his window.

Ep 49

The Taco Theorem

"Are you sure we should not stop for tacos?" Marrow asked. "What if there is no such thing as tacos where we are going? We'll miss out on having them one last time."

"I think we shouldn't stop until we get out of here. Not even for tacos." I glanced at him as we drove. "Unless you're too hungry to continue. When was the last time you were fed?"

"My feeding tube was hooked up yesterday. So it's been...some time, I guess?"

I nodded. I realized that I could not remember how many hours were in one day. *20? 30? 40?* I had no idea...only a fuzzy memory that vanished whenever I tried to examine it too closely. I was certain there were such things as hours and

that they were to be added up to make days, but I couldn't quite recall how it all worked.

"Whoa, Bel," Marrow said, grabbing the wheel and steadying it for me when I swerved. "Maybe we should stop for something to eat after all?"

"No, no. I'm fine. We're fine. I want to keep going. I want to get out."

"When was the last time *you* ate?" he asked me.

"The last time?" When was the last time...? I shook my head. "I think we're almost there, 'Row. We've got to be almost there."

He reached back and nudged Mango awake. She murmured and then shot up. Well, as best she could, considering she was still all tied up. As a result of her misdirected efforts, she flopped to the floor, wedged between the back seat and ours. Marrow removed the cloth from her mouth so she could speak.

"Where do we go, Mango?" I asked, trying to keep calm, though hunger and panic were suddenly making a cocktail in my stomach.

"I don't know. This is insane." Mango struggled against the electronic cords we'd use to secure her. "Let me out. You don't even have to stop driving, just open the door and push me. *Please*."

"We'll let you out once we know where we need to go. You have to know something. About how to get out."

"Why do you think *I* would be told information like that?"

I sighed. "Fine. If you're no use to us, we'll have to kill you. Or else you'll tell the Grades where we are and what we've done."

Mango whimpered in response. "I don't know where to go but I know who does!" She licked her incredibly chapped lips. "You would call him Lǎobǎn."

"Lǎobǎn? *He* knows shit?"

Mango nodded. "He knows shit."

I thought about this for a moment. *Of course*. Of course he knew what was going on Here and There. He always showed up at the worst times, but I'd never actually seen him. Not with my own eyes. I remembered Ratio catching me right before I got home the night Lǎobǎn was laying into my sister. I saw the guy's car. And I saw the after effects of what he did to Confía. I knew people who worked for him. But I had never truly spotted him. Not in all my years in Dime Block.

"How do we find him?" Marrow asked me.

"I have no idea, actually," I said. "Mango, how do we find him?"

"Not entirely sure. But my guess is that if you stopped the car, you'd find him."

"Stop the car?" Marrow inquired.

But it was too late for questions. I slammed on the brakes, and we squealed to a dead, smoking stop in the middle of the open road.

"There," Mango said. "Look."

And sure enough, a ways down the empty, dusty street, framed by trees and blue skies, was a familiar, shiny white car. Parked and waiting.

Ep 50

The Sharpness Of Bel

Bel got out of the car with great speed, and so I did too. She seemed pretty upset, with her eyes narrowed and her lips pressed together tight. Much like Hafiz whenever he discovered a Grade had marred my perfection. I had the sense that whoever was in the white car parked ahead of us would be faced with the same consequences as the Grades who scarred my skin.

Once we were close enough to the car, the person seated inside opened the door and got out. She stood in a short, loose dress, the flower patterns flapping in the stiff breeze, her sandals planted firmly on the road. Dark curly hair whipped over her face.

I thought she was beautiful, but not in the way I found Bel to be beautiful. No one could

match that. There was a sort of sharpness to Bel. Like the fire in the dome where the Grands observed me. Like she could burn us all up at any moment.

Bel only stared at the other girl. Neither of them moved for a long time.

Finally, Bel cracked her lips open and managed a word. "Confía?" she said.

The other girl sighed. "Bellanueva, you are going way off track. This is not supposed to be happening. Not like this."

Tears spilled over Bel's cheeks, but she could not rip her eyes away from the girl. "How could you do this to me?"

"You don't even know what it is I'm doing. What I've done. You are angry for reasons you don't understand."

"So tell me, Confía. Tell me why the only person who ever loved me is literally a lie. Tell me where Lǎobǎn actually is."

"Bel, there is no Lǎobǎn."

Bel shook her head. "Of course there is. Everyone knows about him. He has been ruining the lives of everyone who lives on Dime Block for years. For my whole life. Every single person in East West knows about Lǎobǎn."

"They *know* about him, but he's not real. He's an idea. An effective one, for the most part. Until now. Until you."

Bel's voice raised in volume. "You made up a terrorizing monster? You pretended he forced you to sell your own body? You pretended he hurt you? You pretended he killed dad?"

"No, Bellanueva. You made up a terrorizing monster. We just made him as real as you wanted him to be."

Bellanueva shook her head. "He hurt you, Confía. I saw the blood. I saw the bruises."

"Yes. I was bloodied. And bruised. But there was no Lǎobǎn to do those things."

"Bel," I interjected. "Who is this person?"

Bel turned to me and screamed her response. "She's supposed to be my sister."

"I am your sister," the girl clarified.

"That just makes it worse, Confía! How could you do this to me?"

"Because—"

"Tell me why!"

"Because...I want to go home."

"What does that mean?" I asked. "You have been home all this time."

Confía tried to catch her hair, to keep it from blowing into her face, but it was no use. "Here and There...they aren't our homes. But if we can make Marrow perfect. If we can make a Glimpse undeniably beautiful, maybe we can go back. I just...want to go back. Go home."

"I don't know any home but here," Bel said, scrubbing at her tears. She, unlike her sister, did not care that her hair went wild in the wind.

"That's because you've never been," Confía said. "This whole thing has gotten so out of hand." She closed her eyes, as if she was concentrating on something we couldn't see. Something in her past. Some idea of home we had never conceived of.

"Well..." I spoke up. "We're going. We're going to this 'home' you speak of."

Confía's eyes widened. "You can't."

"I think we can."

"Marrow...if you go...you'll ruin everything. Everything we worked for. We'll have to start all over. Years and years and years of construct and analysis, gone. Lives wasted for nothing. Literally for nothing." She tucked her hair behind her ears in one last attempt to tame it. "Escúchame. I'll make you a deal. You stay, Marrow. Bel can go. She can go wherever she pleases. She can even come back and visit you. But Marrow...please understand. We can't let *you* leave."

Before I could say a word, Bel stepped forward. "Like hell if you think I'm letting any of you come near him again. He's not *yours*. People don't *belong* to you."

"Marrow is not a *person*, Bellanueva. You are throwing your life away—all of our lives, gone—for a Glimpse. A Glimpse of something bigger."

This is when my voice came out of me louder than I ever knew possible. There was an ache in my chest I could not describe and strange throbbing in my head. "I *am* a person."

"Why, Marrow? Because Bellanueva says so? She can't just will you into personhood. That's not how it works. You know nothing about being a person outside of what she's taught you. Nothing at all."

"No," I said. And I took Bel's hand. "I'm a person because I know how to love Bel. And no one can teach that. She taught me fun. She taught me food. She taught me so many things. But that one, I just...know. Because it comes with being a person."

Confía looked like she might have fallen over. "Did you just say...you love—"

"That's what he said," Bel shouted, squeezing my hand. "Now...tell us how to get out of Here and There or—"

"It's that way."

We all turned to find Mango unbound, standing in the street behind us, her finger pointed to the horizon across the small grove of trees we'd passed dozens of times driving between Here and There. She was shaking, it seemed, with her own set of tears staining her brown cheeks.

"It's that way," Mango said again. "But you'd better fucking *run*."

Ep 51

Praying To God Across

We ran. Of all the times I had exerted myself before, this was the most important. I was lucky to match Bel's pace, though I could never move the way she did. When I was taught to run, it was with Hafiz in carefully designed classes. Monitoring was critical and accompanied by critique on the positioning of my head, the length of my stride, the stretch of my abdominals. I had always received extra nutrients on running days so that my muscles developed in a way pleasing to the Grands. When I sweat, it was charted. The quantity, the particular sheen of it, the salt content. My perspiration was rated and measured against the sweat of the other Glimpses.

Mine was said to be pure as crystal. None of that mattered anymore.

When Bel ran, it was different. *She* was different. She moved like something was coming to get her. Like up ahead awaited some sort of salvation. Bel sprinted like she'd been doing it all her life. As though there was no time to be scared if she wanted to survive. I never knew the act of running could be so emotional, so primal. It wasn't meant to be beautiful; it was meant to keep us alive. *Perhaps life and beauty are not complementary.*

Still, I couldn't help but be surprised that Bel was just a bit quicker than me since she, no doubt, lacked the nutritional balance for her body to perform optimally. I loved her for it. I loved her.

We aimed simply for a direction. In some clearing far, far ahead were the few trees on the horizon that seemed to lie dead center between Here and There. I tripped a few times and when I did, Bel stopped to help me up. When she stumbled, I caught her and pushed her forward.

I wasn't sure why Mango told us we needed to run until we heard a roaring behind us. *Something is coming*. Something that wanted to stop us, to take us back. But back wasn't an option for me, and I knew it wasn't one for Bel either. Neither of us turned to see what it was that chased us, but the roaring grew like a ravenous growl shaking the pebbles loose beneath our feet. Like a thousand cars in one had come to life.

There came a point where we could go no further. My lungs burned as I inhaled the dust we'd kicked up. Sweat flooded down into my eyes and blurred my vision, but when I forced myself to see through the sting and turn around, I saw only a column of light racing toward us, big enough to swallow us whole.

And, just ahead of that blaze of white, a car speeding toward us. Confía stuck her head out the open window of that vehicle and screamed. I could hardly make it out, but she kept screaming it, over and over.

Bel deciphered her sister's words before I could. Staring at the chaos that pursued us,

she held onto my arm, digging her nails into my skin.

"What is she saying?" I asked, shouting over the roar of the light. "Bel?"

Bellanueva looked to me, her face caked in the dust that clung to her perspiration. "In español," she yelled back to me. "Recuerda el reloj."

I watched in the most vivid horror as the light ate Confía, car and all. "What does it mean?"

"Recuerda el reloj." Bel had not released my arm. If she squeezed any tighter, she would pierce through my skin and draw blood. "Remember the clock."

Remember the clock? The tower where I'd spent all my days? Why? Remember...what about it? That it exists?

"Should we keep running?" Bel asked, both of us still facing the light, both of us exhausted.

"If you can...we should try."

Bel nodded. "Then we should try."

Hacking on the swirl of dirt and leaves and dust that the light beam kicked up as it seared

across the land, we held on to each other and stumbled forward. *Forward, forward.*

And then I realized what we were doing wrong.

"Bel, no!" I stopped, grabbing onto her. "Not forward. We are trying to go forward but there is no forward. We have to go across."

Bel gasped for air. "Across?"

"God *Across*. Isn't that the saying, Bel? Isn't that what we were taught? We have to go *across*!"

So I held onto her, and she held on to me, and, with the light burning the sides of our faces, we took one more step. Sideways, instead of forward.

Combs

Ep ~~I~~ 52

Land Of The Mouse

At first, I thought the light had eaten us too. That it had burnt us up just like the little version I'd touched, with its dancing yellow heat, in the dome of the Grands. With my eyes closed, I could tell the air around us felt...strange. Humid. And warm.

But there was no pain, except for the burning of my lungs and the stinging of my eyes as I squeezed them shut. I was glad I could still feel Bel in my arms, her heart beating quick against my chest. When she was so close, I knew for certain that she belonged there. That she was meant to be where I was. That she deserved my embrace and more.

"Marrow...Marrow, *look*."

I opened my eyes, looking over Bel's head. I did not know what to think. What to do. Every thought seemed to happen in my mind at once.

More cars than I had ever seen. So many different colors and sizes. They drove at unbelievable speeds on wide, impossible roads. They zoomed and swerved, slamming on brakes with loud horns blaring. Above the cars were pictures of art. But...huge. Bigger than any I had ever seen. The pictures were powered by light and they shifted and changed, depicting varying scenes. One of a man in a sad gray outfit, the word '¿Accidentes?' in big red letters above his head. The image changed to a family of strangers screaming together, all strapped into an odd little car with no roof that ran on a track of some sort. The family's legs dangled in the air seemingly lengths above the ground.

As we stood holding each other, a man pushed past us. He wore many layers of thick, dark clothes, despite the humidity, and pushed a caged cart ahead of him filled with bottles, bags, and other bits of random garbage. He didn't seem to notice us, though we could not stop staring at him.

"Where...what...?" Bel stammered.

"Are we Here?" I asked, still unwilling to let Bel go.

"No. At least...it's not East West. And *definitely* not Dime Block. The smell isn't right. And it's too...pretty. But also, somehow, too ugly."

"And it's not There, that's for sure. It's not pretty enough for Grands. Too disorganized. And I've never seen this many...*things*...in my life. How do people function? How do they find anything?"

"Look at all those buildings, Row. What do you think they're for?"

I turned around to see Bel pointing at clusters of beige-colored buildings. Cars were parked outside of the doors. Maybe one hundred of them, maybe more.

"Should we go see?" I asked her. "Maybe someone can tell us where we are."

"Yes. But...we should be careful. Obviously, we are not supposed to be here." Bel held my hand as we walked toward the buildings on a little strip of sidewalk that kept us apart from the zooming, weaving cars. "Marrow, what was that light thing that chased us? Have you ever seen anything like that There?"

I shook my head. "Bel, I could not have imagined that, not even if Helix dreamed it up for me. What... what was it doing? Your sister—"

"Marrow, I don't know. I don't know anything. Why did she tell us to remember the clock? What could that even mean? Remember what about it?"

"I don't know either, Bel. But, do you think the Grades will come after us?"

"They might. If they can. I don't know if they would have to get through that light thing too. Maybe."

We made it to the buildings and chose one to enter. The doors were made of glass and they slid open without us having to touch them. We both jumped backward at the automation. A waft of cold air met us, relieving our aching limbs. The air smelled clean and sweet. Like chemicals. The fragrance burned my nose, but it was a welcome change from inhaling dust particles.

The lights reminded me of the operating rooms I'd frequented. They were bright and harsh, over-illuminating. And all around the building hung clumps of clothes. Shelves of shoes and bags. People calmly paced the room, touching the clothes and shoes, talking, staring at small rectangles in their palms.

Music floated down from the ceilings. To what end, I couldn't tell. No one danced or sang to it. They all seemed to thoroughly ignore it.

"There." Bel pointed to a woman standing behind a desk. "A book watcher, maybe? She has a computation device. Maybe she can direct us or something."

"Direct us to where?"

"I don't, Row. Food? Water? Or she can tell us where we are. That's probably something we should know, don't you think?"

I nodded. Bel was always good at figuring out what to do. We approached the desk, and Bel cleared her throat.

"Hi, um...Bellanueva Anamaria Morales De Leon. 7,413.52 days old. Born Here, not There."

The woman wielded the longest eyelashes I had ever seen. And she had brown dirt smeared on just below her eyebrows. Black lines ringed around the edges of her eyelids, and her lips were coated in red goo.

"The *hell*?" she said, her brow furrowing. "I only speak English, bruh." She clacked wild, bright blue nails twice the length of mine.

Bel took a breath and tried again. "Where...are we?"

The woman wrinkled her nose, though her voice remained flat. "Orlando, home of the magic mouse."

"What?"

The woman sighed. "Good ole' two ears?"

Bel shook her head. "And it's called...Orlando?"

"Yuh. *Or-lan-do*."

"Would you be able to tell me, perchance, if 'Orlando' is Here or There?"

She blinked her ridiculous lashes. "Is that a trick question?"

"No?"

"Look, if you don't have a question about our merchandise and you don't plan on buying anything, you're going to have to leave."

I decided to give it a try. "Do you have any food or water?"

She stared as if I'd asked her to give me one of her eyeballs. "No, dude. Get out before I call the police."

We turned to leave, and Bel leaned in. "What are 'police' and why do they work for this mouse guy?"

Ep 53

The Thing Near The Garbage Bin

We stepped outside of the strange place with the clothes and shoes because the mouse lady wanted to call on her police. I had only a loose idea of what a mouse was. Some sort of small creature from stories the Grands liked to hear in the evenings. But whatever she meant, it was a threat—that was clear—and we did not need unnecessary attention drawn to us.

"We should have gotten tacos," I mumbled.

Bel sat down on the ground, stretching her legs out. "Yes, Marrow. We should have gotten tacos."

I prepared to sit down beside her, happy to rest my strained muscles, since running from the light had not been easy and my body craved the pulse of vitamins through my feeding tube. But something strange caught my eye. Down the road and near a big green bin. A quick flicker of bright light.

I began walking toward it, but Bel called out.

"Marrow, where are you going?"

"I don't know."

She squinted at me in the bright sun. "You don't know where you're going?"

"Correct. I am just...going over there for a while."

"Oh. Okay, I'll come too—"

"No. You sit and rest."

Bel frowned at me. I could not blame her. It was not usual for me to want to be apart from her. And I did not know what compelled me to keep the flicker of light from her. But I wanted to see what it was on my own, and so that was what I did. I passed by the doors of many rooms that held different clothing and shoes and people and smells. Each door slid open for me, wafting out cold air, but I walked past them all.

I arrived at the large bin. It smelled...dreadful. I peeked inside and realized it was filled to the brim with what had to be garbage. We did not have garbage There, but I had seen enough of it on the streets of Here to identify it without a doubt.

To the right of the garbage bin, another flicker of light. I stepped behind the wall of the building and looked around, but saw nothing. Until, from behind a pile of old cube boxes, a slight shuffle.

"Hello?"

I moved toward the boxes with great caution. I didn't know what dangers awaited in this place. Something that could mar me. Scar me. Or impair my mobility. What would Bel do? She would not hesitate or worry about her beauty. She would simply act. Because it's what needed to be done.

I reached forward and yanked the soggy brown box away, flinging it behind me, my heart screaming in my chest. And then, it all stopped.

"Helix?"

Her brown skin was covered in filth, her dark hair matted and her eyes red and brimming with tears. She wore scrapes on both her knees, her once white clothing torn to tatters.

I hurried to her and dropped to the ground. "Helix, good God Across, what has happened? How did you get here?"

The Glimpse sniffled, wiping her nose with the back of her hand. "Marrow?"

"Yes. Yes it's me." I offered my hand. "Come, Helix, Bel and I will help you."

"Where's Hafiz? Hafiz always helps me. Always. He'll come."

I shook my head. "Lix, Hafiz...he's dead. He's gone. I know that's difficult to hear, but he won't be coming."

She pulled her knees in close to her, scraping at her chin with dirty fingernails. "I'm lost. I'm so very lost."

"Yes. So are we. But we are together again, Helix. You may be lost but you don't have to be alone anymore." I tried to lift her from where she sat, her back against another one of those big green bins. “Come. Bel is good at knowing what to do.”

“I can’t.”

“You can’t? Are you too injured?”

“I cannot let anyone see me. Not like this. Not like this.”

“Helix—”

“No, not like this. Not like this. No one can see me. I won’t matter if they see me.”

I could not keep my eyes from filling with tears. “You will always be beautiful, Helix. You will always matter. It’s okay if they see you.”

But she shook her head. “No. You are wrong, wrong, wrong. I won’t matter.” Then, she pointed upward, tilting her head back so her eyes took in the sunny sky. “Can’t look up forever, Marrow.”

I stood up. “Stay, Helix. I will go get Bel, and she will help. We’ll find food and water. We’ll find a way to help each other. And then...then we can teach you all sorts of things. Fun. And...and love. You’ll see.”

Ep 54

The Perfect Color

"Marrow...there's no one here." Bel spun in a slow circle as she examined the area. "Are you sure you saw a Glimpse?"

"Yes. I'm certain. We even spoke. She looked like she had been here for some time. Do you think...this is where they went when they left the tower? After Hafiz died?"

Bel tried to pull her hair up but realized she had no band on her wrist with which to tie it. Frustrated, she let her dark waves fall back down and settled for shoving them from her face. "It's possible. We made it, so why not the Glimpses? I worry though...what has she been eating? Where has she been sleeping? Did she look...alright?"

"She looked...unlike herself. Her beauty is deteriorating, that much is clear."

"But her health, Marrow. How did that look?"

"What exactly do you mean? Her health? You mean her nutrient balance?"

"Yes. Were her bones showing through her skin more than usual? Did her complexion look vibrant and clear?"

"She showed more bones certainly and she had... little red bumps all over her skin. She was bruised as well. Her hair was matted."

"So she has no caretaker. She's all alone. That's not good, 'Row. We need to find her."

"If we wait, maybe she will come back to this location."

Bel hopped on the balls of her feet as she thought. "No, we can't stay here tonight. We don't know anything about this place, but in East West, nothing good happens at night. We should find some place where we feel at least relatively safe."

"What about those fancy, scented buildings? The mouse lady looked rather comfortable staying in one of those."

"Well, that's a good idea, except she just kicked us out. I don't think we quite fit in."

We paused as a woman waddled past us wearing stilts beneath the soles of her shoes. Her lips smeared in oil and her eyelids weighed down with the glare of metals, she clutched a bag in one hand and a child's wrist in the other. The child stared at an illuminated device, seemingly oblivious that his mother required him to increase his speed or that she even existed.

"Hi," Bel said as the woman took a wide path around us. "Can you tell us where—"

"Freaks," she mumbled, gripping the child more firmly.

"Mom, you're pinching!" the boy squawked, glancing up from the device.

"Just hurry up," she hissed at him. "Get in the store, Skyler."

Bel watched the doors close behind the woman and boy. "So that's a store? It looks like...."

"Like nothing I've seen before and certainly not like any of our stores. But why are the people so...."

"Angry? I don't know. They will definitely crease with all that scowling." It took me a moment to realize Bel was joking. "And that woman almost snapped that boy's arm off trying to keep him away from us." Bel patted her t-shirt. "We look normal, no? Well, I look normal. You look like a god out of an old story. Maybe we need to ugly you up."

Even the words made me want to run. But Bel said them so casually. As if it were as simple as biting into a taco. Or killing an attacker. Or falling in love.

"We could find a car," I said. "We know enough about those. They should be safe."

Bel snapped and winked at me. "Brilliant thinking, Marrow." She put her hands on her hips and surveyed the paved lot of empty cars. "Looks like we have quite the assortment to pick from. Which do you prefer?"

"Brown."

"Really? Brown? Why so boring? There's like...every color you can imagine here. You want a brown car?"

I reached out and touched Bel's cheek, inadvertently wiping off some of the grime and dust that had accumulated there. "Your eyes are brown. And your skin too. And your hair has brown tones when the sun catches it just right. It's a beautiful color to me."

Her cheeks tinted pink, and she cleared her throat, looking away and removing my hand. "A brown car, then. Yes."

"Did I touch you wrong, Bel? Did you not like that?"

Bel stared at me and opened her mouth, but closed it again, not saying anything at all. And then she picked a brown car and went to work.

Ep 55

Back Row Action

We picked a brown car that was bigger than all the rest but smaller than the bus Cyrilus used to take us There from Here. I let Marrow break in—luckily enough, the door being unlocked kept that part from being too tricky—and start it up. I had to admit delinquency looked good on him. He framed his beautiful mouth in such a delicate and devious way whenever he concentrated on a task. I didn't bother pretending not to stare.

When he was finished, I drove the car through the fastest and most crowded streets I had ever seen until we reached a sort of secluded place with enormous shade trees and very few people. A sign read "Altamonte Park."

"We will find food tomorrow," I assured Marrow, sitting beside him in the back row. "I promise. We'll figure this out."

Marrow was quiet for a moment. "I don't think we will."

"Find food tomorrow?"

"Figure this out. I don't think we will."

I wiggled, trying to scoop my hair up and failing to keep it there. '"You think we're going to be lost and confused forever?"

"I think we don't have anyone to fight, which makes winning really difficult. But we will fight anyway until we're through. It's like competing with the other Glimpses, except none of them are here. But I still walk how I am supposed to. I still try to keep from wrinkling." Then he reached over and pulled my hands away from my hair. "Like this. Why do you fight your own hair? Why not let it be how it wants to be?"

"Because I can't think when it's in my face."

The only light fell in slanted through the windows from a flickering streetlamp. Still, I could see the edges of his flawless jaw and the straightness of his elegant nose.

"Why are you thinking so hard?" he asked me.

"Why? Because...I have to think of how to...how to...."

"You have to think. And I have to be beautiful. And neither of us know why or how to stop or who made us start in the first place."

I didn't realize that my hands were back to my hair until Marrow took them down again.

I sighed. "So...you think I'm stuck this way. And you're stuck that way. And we should not try to figure out who did this to us and why?"

"I didn't say we shouldn't try. I just...don't care if we figure it out or not. I want to try. I want to try with you. What could be better, considering the lives we've been given, than to try together to change them? Trying is the part I want to remember. Not whether we succeed or we fail. Bel, I am not saying to stop thinking. I am just pointing out that the thinking is all you can do. Besides...I like to watch you think."

"Well I have some ideas," I started. "I could share them with you? I...suppose I've never said my ideas out loud. Always seemed risky, somehow."

"Like someone might overhear them."

I nodded. "Exactly. But also...that I'm right. It wouldn't be so bad if someone overheard my stupid, ridiculous ideas. But if they were *correct* ideas and someone heard me...I don't know. I'm not sure what I thought might happen, but it scared me enough to keep me quiet."

Marrow stared at me with those deep eyes, the light flickering over his face and giving me just enough time to see him before he faded back into long shadows again. "But you trust *me*?"

"Yes."

He leaned back against the seat and pulled me toward him. "Come closer, then, and tell me your ideas."

I leaned against him, and after a bit of adjusting, ended up with my legs draped over his lap and my head on his chest, his arm tight around me.

"Is this okay?" I asked.

"I have never been more okay. It is like all the okay-ness in the world has found me here."

I chuckled. "Here are the things that keep circling around in my mind. First...fate."

"Define?"

"My abuela—"

"Define."

"My mother's mother, although now I don't know if my mother was even related to me or who my abuela actually was. But she always taught us that fate is a force. A...power. It means things are moving in a certain direction, either toward destruction or toward glory. We don't get to choose."

"If we have no choice, why are we trying so hard?"

"Maybe it's our fate to try. But that's the first thing that sticks out in my mind. The next thing"—the word I'd planned to say next evaporated when Marrow needed a more comfortable place to rest his hand and found my hip.

"What? Why did you stop?"

"No reason." But my entire side tingled with his palm on me, and the ideas I'd wanted to share became slippery. *Festers and fleas, what is he thinking, leaving his hand there*? "So...uh...the other idea...my mom left me a note before she disappeared. She said I'm not wrong."

"Not wrong? About what?"

"Not sure. But sometimes, those words just float to the front of my mind. And when I doubt myself...I remember. I'm not wrong. Like when I knew I needed to leave Here and There. And that I needed to leave with you. That what they did to you was awful and I couldn't just let it happen."

"You're not wrong."

He flexed his fingers, and they tickled against my stomach, causing me to gasp.

"Are you sure this is alright?" Marrow asked. "Is this not how people usually sit together?"

"It...is sometimes how they do it, yes. If they very much like each other."

"I very much like you."

"Then you're doing it right."

"Good. Now, what is another idea you have been holding on to?"

"The clock."

"Ah yes. Recuerda."

"Si."

Marrow's other hand drifted over to my legs, bare beneath my shorts, and he ran his fingers over my skin.

"Bel? Why do you stop talking whenever I touch you?"

Because you know exactly how to touch me.

"It...I...."

"See? You have no words anymore. Am I hurting you?"

I sighed and sat up straighter, pulling my legs away so I was on my knees beside Marrow. "Here, how about I show you. That sound okay with you?"

"You can do anything you would like to me, Bel."

I groaned and rolled my eyes. "See you can't *say* that."

"What? Why not?"

"Because it means...." I shook my head. "Okay, look. Stay still."

And I traced my fingertips along the side of his face, across his jaw, behind his ear, and down his neck, stopping at the hollow of his throat.

"You have to talk while I do it, Marrow."

"Oh. I forgot."

"Should I do it agai—"

"Yes." He turned to face me. "Alright, I am ready."

I retraced the motion, following the same trail along his face until he shivered.

"Marrow...you still said nothing."

He shook his head. "You're right. Words don't come out when you touch me like that."

"Do you like it?"

"I have never felt anything so wonderful." He took my hand and put it to his chest. "I want more."

I blushed. Hard. And Marrow touched my cheek. "It's beautiful when you do that."

"Yeah, well you're doing it too."

"Why? Why is it so...good?"

"Um...hormones."

"Define, Bel."

I shook my head, trying to focus on the Grade definition of physical chemistry. "We—are attracted to each other. And our bodies are reacting to that attraction."

"Oh yes, I know about this. Hafiz taught us. Not with all the smart words like you use, but about the general event."

"Oh. Then...have you...?"

"No. We were not allowed. Have you?"

I paused. What if he did not like my answer? But he was Marrow, and I had no secrets left. "I have, yes. A few times."

He was quiet for a long time. And then he reached up and tugged on my hair. "But they were not like me. They were different."

I laughed. "They were *very* different from you, Marrow."

He did not laugh with me, though. "You would not want to...with someone like me."

I put my hands on his face and did my best to ensure he looked right into my eyes. "Marrow, there is no one like you. And I would. Only, I don't know if *you* would...you're the most beautiful thing...in *existence*."

But he leaned forward and put his lips to mine, pulling away. “Is that how we start?”

I grinned. “A kiss.”

“It’s different than a hug.”

“Claro que sí.”

“Another, then.”

Ep 56

Together Not Together

And this time I leaned in. Before our lips met, I put a hand on his chest. "Wait," I whispered. "Slow down. Slow down with me." And then I kissed him, taking my time. His lips were different from any other guy's. Those kisses had always been equal measures hasty and unmemorable. Something to do when street-lit books were not enough to take my mind off of the pain enclosed behind our front door and the chaos spilling out onto the sidewalks.

Marrow slid his hand to my neck, his fingers touching the edges of my hairline as he leaned into the kiss.

Never, in all my days. An electric current chained itself to my spine, flooding my body with something I had never experienced but recognized at once. *Fate.* It was not merely a force, but a feeling. And the feeling, when I listened to it, moved me forward.

I plucked his lips with mine, more and steadier, until I thought maybe I would damage his sensitive skin.

"More is good," he mumbled. "More."

But still, I was concerned, so I kissed his neck instead. His skin was undeniably smooth, as if I were the first person to ever touch him.

Suddenly, he pulled away. He seemed breathless, and I feared I was right, that somehow I had hurt him. Or...or offended him, which would have been so much worse.

"What's wrong?" I asked him.

"Nothing. Nothing is wrong."

"Marrow—"

"You care how I feel. That's all. I was trying to understand why you keep hesitating. But then it came to me. Everyone in my life—Hafiz and the Glimpses and the Grades—they have cared about me yes, but only about how I look. How I function. And you...you care about how I feel. About...how I am. About what feels good to *me*. In my body. In my mind."

"That's what happens when you love someone, 'Row. I want you to feel good. Not just for me, but for you."

"That's...unbelievable. Bel, why? Why love me?"

I tried to keep the emotion from welling up in my voice and causing my words to falter. "Because you're wonderful. I don't know what else to say. You deserve to feel as good as you are."

Marrow thought about this, his perfect head angled just slightly downward. "You deserve to feel as good as you are," he repeated.

Then he put his hands on my waist. "You know better than me, Bel. Show me how."

So I pulled his shirt over his head and let his long black hair hang down his back so I could lace his chest with my lips, then my tongue. His breath caught when I made my way down, but then he stopped me.

Marrow pulled my shirt over my head and kissed my neck, my chest.

"What are you doing? Why...did you stop me?"

"You deserve to feel as good as you are."

"Marrow, let me—"

"No, Bel, it's my turn. All you've done is make me feel good. You showed me life. You taught me how to be a person. Now it's my turn to show *you*."

This made me uncomfortable. Maybe because I did not know how to take something like that and believe it. I was no one. Not a Grade or a Grand or a Glimpse. But I couldn't tell Marrow I didn't deserve it. I couldn't tell him that I shouldn't have the attention and affection I had been waiting to give to him.

"Teach me how, if you want. But I'm going to be the one to do it," he said, sensing my hesitation.

"I don't need to teach you."

"So I may?"

I took a deep breath and moved so that I straddled him. "No," I said. "We go together."

It took a moment or two or five of us figuring out how to move together, how to undress completely in the tight space of the car, how to keep from falling between the seats.

"Me on top," I said after our fourth adjustment, each one better than the last.

"Ready?" Marrow chuckled, out of breath over me.

"No." I pushed on his chest. His skin had grown warm, and his heart beat heavy against my palms. I was afraid that if he touched my chest again, he would know how much my heart outpaced his. I was afraid he would know how much I wanted him.

"We can stay like this?" he asked, lifting me by the waist and taking a gentle bite of the skin of my abdomen and then twisting so he looked down at me.

"You'll be doing all the work…."

"Good." He kissed me again and again, moving lower each time. "I think I have got it now. You can leave it to me."

I gasped, my back arching. He was not wrong. He knew exactly what to do. "I thought…together…."

But Marrow ignored me, and I no longer had what it took to say anything at all.

Ep 57

The Favorite Part So Far

I remembered Hafiz used to look at me in this particular way. As if I was the most beautiful thing he had ever seen. But also as though he hated me for what I was not. His job was to adjust. To make me more beautiful. To interpret the desires of the Grands and to form me to match. If I could not be formed, I would be broken. If I could not be repaired after that, I would be removed.

"Do not worry," he would say to me. "If you worry, you will crease. And wrinkle. And then your beauty will vanish, along with everything we have worked for."

Not once had Bel ever shown concern about my creasing. Instead, she dug her nails into the skin on my back. She did not mean to do this. I do not even think she was aware of her actions. But when I moved forward and reached inside her, I wanted nothing more than the pain and destruction she offered. In many ways, I hoped she would tear me apart.

Because Bel was the first person who refused to let me be perfect.

The longer we stayed close, the more I enjoyed it. The more I felt like it was exactly what I was supposed to be doing. Fate, Bel would call it.

"Are you sure," Bel mumbled, biting my shoulder, then my neck, then my lip, "you're okay with this?"

"No more asking," I told her. "Do whatever you want."

"Marrow—"

"I want you to do whatever you want. Anything you want."

But it seemed what she wanted was exactly the same as what I wanted. By the time I realized my heart was going to flood my body and, certainly, I would die, the car was too hot for us to breathe.

"Everything..." I said. I didn't have anything else I could say to her. Only that everything in me had suddenly become aligned. And that as long as I had Bel, as long as she let me touch her the way I touched her, as long as she allowed me inside of her, near her, closer than I had ever been with any person...I would be more than beautiful. I would be *alive*.

"You're crushing me," Bel gasped.

She was so much smaller than I expected. And softer. And stronger.

I made an attempt to sit up so I would no longer make her uncomfortable, but Bel wrapped her arms and legs around me and held me close.

"Not yet," she said.

"But...I do not want to crush you."

She sighed, her eyes closed. "Never mind that. I don't want it to end yet."

"I can sit up and hold you, if you would like that. Or you can crush me. I am so much larger than you. I don't think it would bother me."

"You want...to hold me for *longer*?"

"What else could I possibly hope for?" I took her body and pulled her on top of me, spinning so I was on my back. I ignored the belt buckles pressing into my spine and instead focused on the slowness of just being, trailing my hands along the curves of her. The world went quiet. Even more than that...it listened. To what it listened, I could not say for sure. But I knew it was epic. I knew it was timeless. "This is my favorite part so far."

She nuzzled her cheek against my chest. "No one has ever held me after. It's just...not something we do Here. It's not something we prioritize. Being close. Going slow."

"That was...slow?"

She laughed, and I curled my hands in her hair. "Usually I was up against a wall in a minute. Done in two."

"And you...prefer that over what we did?"

She laughed hard enough to shake the whole car. "No, Marrow, I definitely preferred us taking our time."

"Taking our time," I repeated.

Bel sat up straight. The light outside the windows bounced against her bare breasts, replaced just as quickly with long shadows. "Taking our time. Marrow. Taking. Our. Time."

I ran my finger down the center of her abdomen. "We can do it again. I really would not mind."

"No, no. Marrow. They are *taking our time*."

"You mean...literally?"

"Yes. Literally."

"Who? How? Bel, I have no idea what you are talking about."

"I don't know who. The Grades? The Grands? The...the...."

"How does someone *take* time? What does that mean?"

"The clock. Something to do with the clock. The tower. The focal point of the whole...everything. It's not to measure time. It's to measure the time we have left, Marrow." She hopped off of me. "Come on. We need to go."

"Go? It's dark out! And we are...we are very naked. Go where?"

"Quick, Marrow." And she peered out the window as if the strangest of notions had crossed her mind. "We need to talk to someone who lives...*Orlando*."

Ep 58

The Way To Play

"Are we not taking the car?"

"Leave the car," Bel said, zipping up her shorts as we walked. She stopped and smacked my chest. "Where's your shirt? You have to put that on!"

"It's in the car...."

"Go get it, Marrow. No one will be able to form words if you're half-naked. How will we talk to anyone? You'll blind them with your beauty. Go, go."

I fetched the shirt just as car lights flashed through the window. I pulled it over my head and hurried back to Bel, my heart lurching. *What if it's the Grades? What if they found us? What if they remove Bel?*

I ran over to her to find her speaking with people who looked nothing like Grades. They were Bel's age. And in every way, it seemed, far from the beautiful Glimpses I'd spent most of my time with. Some of them had rings in their noses and lips. Others had markings on their arms and necks. None of their hair was what I would have considered normal. Some had shaved heads. Others wore tresses of purple and pink.

Some hung their limbs out over the open back of their car. Others were crammed in the front behind the steering wheel.

"You can bring your boyfriend if you want," one of the boys said. The guy stuck his tongue out and winked at Bel. "Wouldn't mind if you left him behind though. You're hot."

"I'm *hot*?"

The boy wrinkled his nose. "Are you guys foreign or something?"

"Sure," Bel said. "We're foreign or something."

"Hot. You look good. Like...I want to take your clothes off."

I did not expect a fire to erupt inside of me, but suddenly I wanted to hurl a scalpel through the boy's smug face.

"Ew," Bel said, her face blank.

But I was not blank. "Bel will be the only one taking her clothes off. And if you think it is fun to embarrass her about her body, I will tear you apart. I am very accustomed to being torn apart. I believe I would be very good at it."

The boy clamped his mouth shut, and the others in the car went quiet. "Dude, I was just playing around."

"Play differently," I said.

Bel put her hand on my arm. I assumed she did it to calm me, but it only made me more upset. She was too good for anyone to look at her the way the boy dared to.

"Alright, alright. Protective asshole boyfriend. Whatever, man. But seriously, you guys should come." He pointed to the cluster of trees a ways beyond our van. "Through there. We have all the stuff."

What stuff? And they had...all of it?

The car drove off with the people inside whooping and wailing and laughing, music blasting at an extreme volume—music that sounded like garbage bins colliding and a hundred surgical drills going off at once.

Bel grinned at me once they'd left. "Play differently, huh?"

"It is not something for laughing at."

"I'm not laughing at them. I'm laughing at you, 'Row."

"I'm not being funny."

But she beamed anyway, stepping toward me and wrapping her arms around my waist. Her body pressed firmly against mine, and I felt my breath catch. "Alright. I won't laugh."

"He did not look at you like you deserve to be looked at."

"No. I suppose he didn't. Not like you do."

"Precisely." I sighed, kissing her forehead. "Do we have to go to where they went?"

"Yes. I need to ask them questions. And they, unlike the women at the store where we first arrived, are at least willing to speak with us."

Ep 59

Happiest Of Days

Marrow held my hand as we parted the last of the low-lying branches and entered the clearing where the boy had mentioned he and his friends would gather.

There were maybe twenty or thirty young people. I would have said they were our age, but technically Marrow was ageless. The partiers laughed, bumping shoulders, dancing to the low rumbles of the worst music I had ever heard.

"What is this noise?" I asked, covering one of my ears. I would have covered both ears if Marrow didn't have a death grip on my other hand.

Some girl overheard and grinned, banging her head so her hair flopped over her face. "Death metal forever!"

Death metal? Is this their idea of music? Metal scraping against metal until someone dies from the sheer sound of it?

"I do not like this particular idea of fun," Marrow shouted near my ear, though it was still difficult to hear him. I knew he was serious, but his breath tickled my neck and made me want to curl up in his lap all over again. I began to question leaving the soft darkness of the back seat of our car. "How long must we stay here with them?"

"Until they answer my questions. We can figure this out, Marrow. I know we can. We just have to try."

I noticed everyone in the clearing had a bright red cup in hand. So we made our way over to the table where they were stacked. I asked for one, and the boy behind the table rolled his glittery eyes and held out an empty hand.

"Why are his lips so greasy and colorful?" Marrow said to me. "Is he...is it his health? Does he have no caretaker?"

"No, it's their idea of beauty, I think." And then I shushed him and shook my head at the boy. "We have no gol."

"What?"

I pointed to her open hand. "We can't pay you."

"Then you can't drink, b."

"B?"

He scoffed and retracted his hand. "Find another spot to plague."

We left the cup boy and found the one who had invited us to come over in the first place. He was happy to see us. Made sense, as this must have been their version of Happyday. I was surprised they hadn't started on the roasting of the pig. Maybe there were no pigs in Orlando.

Instead, they ate cheese-topped arepas out of cardboard boxes, their mouths flopping open as they chewed the arepas and sipped from the red cups.

"Want me to buy you a drink?" the boy who happened to be playing just a bit differently asked me.

"No, she does not want a drink," Marrow snapped.

The guy smirked at Marrow's response. "I wasn't asking you."

I squeezed Marrow's hand in mine and nodded my head toward the arepas. "See if you can get us some food, mi amor."

"Pizza's free," the guy said, stepping aside so Marrow could get by. Once Marrow was gone, he sized me up. "So...you want some stuff? Guy you're with doesn't look like he wants to party."

"What's the mouse?"

He wrinkled his nose. "Huh?"

"This is Orlando. The land of the mouse. What's the mouse?"

"Oh...Mickey Mouse? You wanna go to Disney World?"

"There are more worlds here?" This complicated things greatly.

"No. What? Oh, are you already high? That makes a lot more sense."

"Oh, *drugs*? Yes. Sure. I am already high. Thanks. So"—I pointed at his outfit—"do you get those clothes at the store?"

He glanced down at his ordinary shirt and ordinary jeans. "Yeah. Why? You like?"

"No."

He laughed. "You're insane."

"Do you know anything about the clock?"

"About...about clocks?"

"About *the* clock. The tower. The clock."

"Nah. But we can go over there and you can sit on my lap. Anywhere, really."

"Shut up, Chad." A girl walked over to us, her arm around Marrow's waist. 'Row's face was one of complete confusion and utter embarrassment. "These guys need help, not invitations to the worst ride in the City Beautiful."

The...City Beautiful?

Ep 60

An Important Definition

"That's what's on the sign. City Beautiful." The girl turned to the guy, Chad, who, after all, was playing exactly the same. "Chad, these guys have no place to stay."

"So?"

"So, I'm going to be nice and take them home."

"You can't *take them home, Tia*. You don't know them."

"So you can ask a stranger for a random lap dance, and I can't offer them showers and a couch at my mom's?" She reached out and shoved her palm into his face. "You're the worst."

She set her jaw straight and lowered the most beautiful head of brown curls I had ever seen. Then, she looped her arms in ours, me on one side and Marrow on the other, and led us away from the party.

"Ignore him. You guys have been through enough. Monroe here told me all about it."

I glanced up and over at Marrow, and he shrugged, his eyes wide. "I...he told you everything?" I stuttered.

"Yeah, babe. You two are so cute. Star-crossed lovers. Running from the Man. Parents be damned. School be damned. And...sometimes you just need a leg up. You just need a break, you know? So I'm gonna be that break. And you'll love my mom. She's the best. *Ever*. That's why I don't even bother to eat this dank-ass forest pizza. She has jerk chicken cooked and ready. Pigeon peas and rice. Corn on the cob."

"I am assuming that is all food. And food sounds good to me," Marrow said. "I am not used to being hungry for this long. Truly, I am not used to being hungry at all."

"I'm mean when I'm hungry, bro. I feel you." The girl nodded her head slowly.

"You *feel* me?"

"Monroe...I *feel* you." She steered us back the way we'd come and toward a beat-up old car. "This is my ride. You guys have bags or anything we need to pick up?"

I shook my head. "No, just us."

"Dang. You really do need some help, huh. Okay, in we go, in we go."

We slid in, and she took off down the dark road.

"Um...hey, who are you?" I asked her.

"Oh, my bad. Tianna. Tianna Green. 407 born and raised." She weaved in and out of the lines of cars.

I almost choked on nothing. "You're 407 *days old*?"

"What the—no! Why would you think...no, it's my area code. For the phone."

I just nodded my head and pretended I knew what an area code was and why it was responsible for her birth and how she was raised. Marrow held my hand, and we watched the lights outside of the car blur by us as we left the trees and found ourselves among houses and stores.

"The lights are different here," Marrow whispered in my ear as he pulled me close. And then he pressed his lips to my temple. I shivered, melting into him, letting him hold me up with his impeccable posture.

"You guys are adorable, you know," Tianna said, glancing back at us in her rearview mirror. "In a special kind of way. Like...characters in a story, if you get what I mean. Or a movie."

I was too tired to ask her what a movie was. Or to think for too long about what sort of terrible love stories she'd read in her books that reminded her of us.

"I love to read," I mumbled, sleep drawing me even closer than Marrow.

"You do?" Marrow asked.

"Mm. Under the streetlights."

And when we woke up, we were parked outside of a nice beige building, the apartments stacked almost as tall as the clock tower.

Tianna led us inside, and her mother woke up and scooped puddles of creamy chicken onto bowls of fluffy rice. We drank sweet purple juice, and Marrow literally fell out of his seat when he burped for the first time in his life.

"God Across, eating is such a strange thing," he said as I helped him back up.

"Well, you kids must be exhausted," Tianna's mother said, her hands on her thick hips, her full lips pursed as she took a good look at us. "We'll have to figure out what to do with you in the morning."

"Ma," Tianna said, her pretty features scrunched with concern. "You're not going to turn them in, are you?"

"In the morning, we'll all sit down and talk it out. Then we'll make a decision, Tia. They're too young for me to just send them out there all alone. It's dangerous in this big ole' world."

"But they have each other. They're not alone."

"Two kids on the run are still two kids, Tianna. Even if they're old enough to wander, I need to know they're going to be okay. That there isn't a family or two hunting for them. Missing them. Heartbroken. Now, all of you. Off to sleep. Monroe, Bel, you two can take the couch." And then she smiled. "Unless you want to snuggle with Tianna, Bel. She still likes for me to tuck her in."

I took a step closer to Marrow and away from Tianna and her mother. "What's that?"

"What's what, child?"

"Tucking her in. Sounds...alarming."

"Oh, I've been tucked," Marrow offered. "It's not the worst procedure. They pull the skin back and snip—"

"No, no, no, good lord! Not that kind of tucking," Tianna interrupted. For some reason, both Tianna and her mother let their arms fall. Their countenances followed. "No one has ever tucked you in, Bel?" Tianna asked.

"I wouldn't know. Never heard of it."

"It's when a parent or a loved one...they make sure you're settled in bed and happy for the night. They check to see if you're comfortable or if you need more comfort. And they say something sweet to you. Usually about how much they love you. And they wish you a good night. Pull the blanket up over you. Maybe kiss your forehead."

Marrow spoke up. "And this is your daily reward, Tianna? Do you get it for being beautiful?"

Tianna blinked. "You can't earn a tuck. It's just what people do when they love you. *Because* they love you."

"How many of them do you get?"

Tianna and her mother exchanged pitying looks. "You get as many as you want. Until you feel confident enough in life and don't need them anymore."

I shook my head. "I've never heard of anything like that."

"It's a custom, I suppose. Maybe it doesn't happen where you're from." Ti's mother paused. "Where are you from, Bel?"

"I'm from Here."

"Oh. Well...."

"But you're not from Here, right?" I asked Tianna's mom.

She flashed a beautiful white smile. "From Haiti. But Tia was born in Orlando. First generation." She popped her head into a closet door and returned with a pile of blankets and pillows. "Here you go. You two get comfortable. And in the morning, we'll decide whether we need to involve the police or not."

I squeezed in next to Marrow on a thing called a couch, and we stared at the flickering lights of the rectangular screen in the center of the room until we fell asleep.

Ep 61

Flickering Lights

I took comfort in the fact that Marrow's heart beat against my cheek. I adjusted, wiping at the puddle of drool I'd left on his flawless amber skin, pretending I did not want to trace the curves of his abdominal muscles with my sullied fingers.

Marrow didn't snore when he slept. Instead, he exhaled like a dream had taken him captive. I wondered if Glimpses dreamed at all. If there was a nightmare in his head more vivid than the one we'd lived every day at home.

I kept from stirring so he could get his rest. After all, we'd gotten very little sleep since we maybe murdered Ratio and definitely murdered Cyrilus. That left me little to do but to stare at the flickering screen in the center of the room. The device was positioned to draw attention to it, but unlike a computation device, it simply showed images. There was no input system, and it didn't seem to pull up any information.

Why do they have one of these in their house?

There seemed to be some story being told in the images. A rather angry man was mass murdering other rather angry men. I couldn't tell which was supposed to be the hero. Of all the stories I'd read, none seemed to be so...violent.

In between the stories were random flashings of different tales. They were poorly told. The plots were miniscule and half-starved. A child eating a bowl of mush, smiling from ear to ear, his mother ruffling his golden curls. A dog running and a man kneeling to greet him, then the dog eating its own bowl of mush.

But something about the little stories made my stomach clench and my breath catch. The people—they were not *happy*. Not really. They smiled, but it seemed to me they were being tortured, forced to act. The mothers and children embraced like strangers. The dog paused before he leapt into the waiting arms of the man as if it were obeying a command. The actions were not genuine. They were lies.

Just like the art on the walls of the room the Grades kept me in while I worked for them. Fake stories for the purpose of...well, I couldn't make out the purpose of such things.

And then...another little story. This one consisted of an image of a tall brown building with many windows.

A smiling woman—she reminded me of a Grade—s-tood outside the building, one hand on her hip, her smooth blonde hair pulled back from her face, and a large white smile matching her Grade coat.

Behind her, the name of the building on a white sign. But I could hardly make it out. It wasn't until the letters themselves appeared in stark yellow on the screen that I could decipher what the building was called.

LAWRY ASSOCIATION OF BEAUTY AND NEUROSCIENCE

I sat all the way up. Lawry Association Of Beauty And Neuroscience. **L.A.O.B.A.N.**

I had to put my hand over my heart to keep it from melting inside me. *How? How can this be happening? How can this exist out here in Orlando?*

"Marrow." I nudged him awake, my eyes tearing up at the sweet sound of his groan of denial.

"Must I be adjusted?" he mumbled.

***So he does dream after all.* I leaned to him and kissed his forehead. "Wake up, Marrow."**

His eyes fluttered open, and as soon as he saw me, he sighed and smiled. "It's you."

"It's me."

"You look worried." I could tell he surveyed my face, searching out the beginnings of wrinkles. But he caught himself in the act and said noth-

ing about my skin or its flaws. "What's wrong, Bel? Did you not sleep well?"

"I did sleep. But then—"

"Did you want to be close again? Because I certainly would not mind that."

I grinned. "That was good, wasn't it?"

"But that's not what you were going to say. What is it? What's wrong?"

I pointed to the screen. "I found Lǎobǎn."

Marrow sat up, changing his posture to match mine. "You did? In that device?"

"It just showed me images, 'Row. He's not actually in there. But I saw an image of a building, and the sign on it was an acronym for his name. And Confía was right. He's not a him at all."

"An...acronym? What is an acronym?"

"Marrow, I think Lǎobǎn is not a person. It's an organization. And that organization has a building in Orlando. That's why we couldn't find any answers Here or There. We were looking for a person and we were looking in the wrong place."

Ep 62

Looking In The Right Place

Bel and I both felt odd about taking Tianna's car after she had been so kind to us. Without the food she and her mother had shared, we would have had one hungry night. But it was time to go, so we went.

We took a random car from another house, and Bel drove us through an area with tall buildings and busy streets. It reminded me of home, except it smelled like refuse and urine, and no glittering Grands walked to and fro.

"You think we'll find answers, Marrow?" Bel asked.

I was not too sure why she wanted answers so badly. Truly, I just wanted her. But if they were important to Bel, I would make answers important to me. "We'll find something, I'm sure."

I wondered how she knew where she was going. Eventually, though, she stopped at a station for gas and asked someone for directions.

"We're pretty close, actually," Bel said, getting back into the car. "And look, I stole this for you."

I wrinkled my nose. It was a drink in a brown bottle. "What is it? It smells so *terrible*."

"Cerveza." She pushed the bottle into my hands. "Beer. Try it. It's disgusting but it's worth it."

I took a sip of the frothing liquid and gagged. It burned my nose, my throat, my eyes. "Oh Bel, this is awful. Just awful. Why would you drink this willingly?"

She laughed until tears squeezed from the corners of her eyes. "My dad used to hide them in the house and drink them at night when he was frustrated. I would steal them and take them with me when I read. For relaxation."

"This is what you drink for comfort?" He put his hand on his belly as a belch erupted. "It *hurts*."

She snatched the bottle from me and swallowed some of the beer. "It hurts good, though, doesn't it?"

I shook my head. "No Bel. It hurts bad."

While she drove, I pushed the buttons on the car until music poured through us. This music

was different than the clashing and scratching of the sounds we'd heard in the woods the night before. The notes lifted and fell, swung and tilted with grace. I put my hand out the window and imagined the air currents were as alive as the song, as Bel and me. When we arrived at a tall brown building, Bel didn't bother to park the car in any of the clearly designated spaces.

"We'll just take another if we have to," she explained. "This place has more cars than people. They probably won't even notice if one is gone."

We both stood outside the building. I could not tell Bel why I was so nervous, that I held my breath because I did not know the answer. But she must have known what I did not because she slipped her hand in mine and pressed her interlaced fingers tight.

"We're going to figure it out," she said.

"Bel...why?"

She shook her head. "I don't know why. All I can think of is...I want you safe, Marrow. So we need answers."

"How will going into L.A.O.B.A.N. keep me *safe*?"

"I don't know. I really don't know. But—"

I kissed the back of her hand. "I trust you. And I don't care what we do as long as I get to hold your hand and be a person with you."

She nodded. And then we both walked in through the self-opening front door.

In the front of the chilled room, a woman with long eyelashes and chalky skin smiled at us. "Good Morning and Welcome to L.A.O.B.A.N. How may I help you?"

How can she help us? It was a good thing Bel would do the talking.

"We need...answers. Please."

The woman blinked, her smile unwavering. "Well, I bet I have some of those. What's the question, hun?"

"Who's in charge?"

The woman chuckled. "Why, that would be Mr. Lawry, of course. His name is on the building, sweetie."

"We need to speak with him."

I suddenly remembered throwing a scalpel into the forehead of the Grade threatening us There. Cyrilus, Bel had called him. I wondered if this was what Bel had in mind for this Mr. Lawry person. I couldn't be certain, but if he threatened Bel like Cyrilus had, I would stop him. That was a simple enough truth.

"You'll have to make an appointment. He's a very busy man."

"Then make the appointment."

The woman's smile began to slip. "Have a seat. I'll see when he's next available." She gestured to plush chairs. They reminded me of the ones in the room outside the testing area, where all the Glimpses would wait to discover who would be sent to a life in Grit and who would continue in their beautification process for the Grands.

We sat, and the woman began speaking into devices and clacking her fingers on her desk. After twenty or so minutes, I had the feeling we were being ignored. I was about to suggest leaving to Bel when something shiny caught my attention. There it is again. A small flash of light.

Helix.

Ep 63

The Matter Of Mattering

The flash came from a little hallway with a sign above it reading 'Restroom'. Why this Orlando had a room entirely for rest was beyond me. The people did not seem too frantic here, nor did they seem particularly overworked. But perhaps the reason for their relaxed, though grumpy, demeanors was a direct result of having rooms set aside just for resting. To be fair, my rest had always been scheduled. Without it, beauty could not be achieved. But with Bel that rest had been stripped thin. I did not mind being tired. It meant I was doing something worth doing. It meant I was with her.

"Bel, I will be right back," I said.

"Be right back? 'Row, where are you going?"

"To the restroom."

"The what?"

I pointed. "That."

"What's in there?"

"Rest, I am assuming. I'll be back. You wait for the lady to tell us when we can see Mr. Lawry."

"Alright," Bel said, biting her bottom lip. "It's a bit suspicious that there's a whole room dedicated to resting. If you're not back in time for our appointment, I'll run in and get you. But Marrow...please be careful."

I nodded. "I will rest as carefully as I can."

And I hurried into the room. To my surprise, it was filled with white toilets and many sinks. *What a strange way for the people of Orlando to rest*. But everything about Orlando was a little strange to me. From the way everyone seemed annoyed to have to speak to one another to their colorful lips and flabby skin.

"Helix?" I whispered. "Helix, is that you?"

Helix lurched out of one of the stalls and grabbed me by the shirt, pulling me in and clamping her hand over my mouth. She was skin and bones, her hair ragged and matted and filthy, her eyes puffy and red and running.

"Marrow...what are you doing *here*?"

I had to remove her hand for her to hear my answer. "We are looking for ans—"

"Run away from this place. Now."

"Is it...is it dangerous?"

"Go now. Out that window."

I did not even look to see where the window was located. "I will not go out any windows without Bel, Helix. I have to get her first."

"No, no, no, no. You walk out of this restroom, and they will have you. They will take you. They will add you up and calculate you, Marrow. They will take *me* from you. And they will call it beautiful. Don't you want to matter? Don't you want *me* to matter?"

I put my hands on Helix's bony shoulders, trying to calm her. "I want to matter, Helix. Whatever that means. But I won't matter without her."

"Listen to me. *Listen to me*, Marrow. Forget the clock. Forget the clock. Forget fate. Forget the girl. Just"—and she put her dirty hands on my face—"just don't forget me."

"I'll remember you, Helix."

"You *won't*!" And big tears dripped down her cheeks, cutting paths through the grime on her skin. "You forgot all the others. So many others.

You will forget me, and I won't *matter*. I won't matter anymore. Why can't you understand what I mean?"

I took her hands away from my face. Her fingers felt brittle, her skin flaking and blistering. "Stay here and wait, Helix. I will go with Bel to talk to Mr. Lawry. And we will get answers. We will figure things out. Then, I promise I will come back here for you, and I'll show you everything I've learned. Hugging, Helix. And having fun. Murdering, which we will have to be careful with. Plus eating. Helix, you will love eating. We will get some tacos. And...and a beer. It hurts, but in a good way. Trust me."

Ep 64

Susan Calls Reinforcements

"Good morning," a man said. He wore a matching top and bottom set. The material was thick and made of the starkest black I had ever seen. It rivaled even the richness of Marrow's hair, but still was not quite as rich. Nothing could quite match that depth of darkness.

"Hey," I answered, slouching in my seat and trying not to glance at the restroom from which Marrow had still not emerged. "Are you Mr. Lawry?"

"I am indeed." He spoke from a doorway, leaning on the frame in an effort to look casual. But I could tell he was faking it. Like Ratio whenever he feigned confidence. Or Confía when she pretended everything was alright after a

long day. His very posture was a lie. "And you are...?"

"I'm waiting for my friend. He's resting."

"Resting?"

I pointed to the room. "In there. He'll be out any second."

"Ah, I see." The man straightened. He wore a plain but large nose, a manicured mustache, and beady pale blue eyes. "Why don't you come on back, and we can send for your friend to join us?"

"No, I'll wait." And then I stood to my feet, my stomach clenching. My skin crawled, just like it used to when I sat down for Grade tests. "I'm actually going to go check on him—"

"Suit yourself. But you go in there, and he will undoubtedly die."

I stopped mid-step and turned to face the unassuming man with the balding hairline. "What did you just say?"

"Well, he won't die. Not like you or I would. But he will cease to exist if you don't start listening to what you're told. If you don't start doing what's required of you, Bellanueva Anamaria Morales De Leon. 36.72 days old. Born Here, not There."

I blinked at him. My mind raced much too fast, and I felt my knees wobble as if I would fall. "I'm—no, I'm not—that's not my age."

"I keep time differently than you. But you already figured that part out, didn't you. The clock. You know it's *something*. Something important. But you don't know what." He sighed, rubbing a meaty hand over his sparse hair. "When they flagged you for your intellect markers being too high, I should have removed you. But...well, you get results, Bellanueva. So I kept you in."

"What are you talking about? Kept me *in*? Intellect markers? You wanted to have me removed for being too smart? Grades are supposed to be smart." I motioned to the desk, the front door, the restroom. "What is all this? How did it get here? Orlando, and all these people and these cars? What is this?"

"This is the real world, Bellanueva."

I realized I was not breathing, but also could not bring myself to remedy that fact. "What?"

"Orlando. It's one of many millions of real cities. There are eight billion people on the planet.

But those in Here and There don't count. They can't count."

I shook my head. "You can't decide who counts as real. Who even are you?"

"Legally, I'm your caretaker. You're my intellectual property. And my responsibility." The man pointed to the restroom. "And the Glimpse? Well, I made it. And seeing that you've been dead-set on unmaking it, I think you should listen for once and come with me. You'll be reunited with it soon. Once you understand what's happening."

I took a step away from Mr. Lawry. "There is nothing you can say that would convince me to leave Marrow. Not even for a moment."

The man sighed. "Susan, go ahead and signal the guards then. Have them take her to Room 11."

"Right away, Mr. Lawry."

"And have them keep the Glimpse in holding until we're ready. But be careful with him, as always. Extra careful. Not a scratch. We have a lot of work to do."

Ep 65

Room 11 With Mr. Lawry

The room was decidedly less impressive than the average Grade lab, but it was just as easy to trash. After what felt like half a day of snapping screens and clobbering equipment with chairs, I crumpled to the floor.

"Let me out!" I cried, but my voice was only a hoarse whisper. "Let me see him. What are you doing to him?" I could only imagine Marrow with his fingers disassembled or his jaw wired closed. I could only imagine him in agony with no one to give half a damn about his pain or his needs. I crawled over and tried the door for the hundredth time, wishing it would yield to my efforts. "Please!"

"Why don't you take a seat, Bellanueva, and we can have a nice chat?" The voice of Mr.

Lawry came floating through the air over some auditory system. "I would love for it to be in person, but I also would love to avoid being ripped to shreds by your fingernails and teeth. Think you can calm down long enough? Reduce the feral?"

A tear slid down my cheek unbidden, and I scrubbed it with my arm. I was too tired to be feral anymore. Too tired to bring myself to hurt Mr. Lawry. To throw another chair. To keep from crying. "Please don't hurt him anymore." *Why did we come here? Why did I insist on knowing the truth? We could have run. We could have lived. If there are eight billion people in the world, Lawry never would have found us.*

The door clicked open, and the man came in carrying his own chair. He sat in it, facing me, and crossed his legs, indifferent to the disaster I'd wrought. "Are you hungry, Bellanueva?"

"No." It was a lie, of course. I had been hungry every single day of my life.

"There is a reason we placed you in Grit. A reason you've been deprived of the many

things you've needed. Food and clean clothing. Familial stability and a sense of general safety."

"I want Marrow."

"And you'll see him soon. But first you need to understand a few things."

"Please—" *Too tired to understand. Too tired.* I closed my eyes and imagined falling asleep on Marrow's chest. His breath slow and steady, his skin slick with sweat and perfect and warm beneath my cheek.

"You are one of the first. One of the first to truly be born Here. Not There. Not anywhere else. You see, we started this program, this lab, this *idea* decades ago. Our world—the real world—operates on consumption. Supply and demand of goods. I know that's difficult for you to understand because Here and There are not that way, by design, but in this world, we sell and we buy. And there really isn't anything else, Bellanueva. If this cycle breaks, people will suffer. They will literally die in the streets. We rely on the system of consumption. We need it.

"So...the notion came about that if we learn how to sell more effectively, people will be able to buy more easily. And we can *direct* what they buy so that they buy products from sellers who really *value* selling. So the cycle is more likely to remain unbroken for years and years to come."

I interrupted the man. "What does your buying and selling have to do with me? Or with Marrow? Leave us out of it."

"That would be quite ridiculous. You were designed *for* this system."

"You are buying and selling us?"

"No, Bellanueva, no. We created a group. A group that allows us to flawlessly predict what people want to buy. Because we have identified beauty itself. It is ever changing, of course, but we are also flexible. Decades ago, this group consisted of volunteers. Volunteers who believed in the raw science of experimentation. And then it grew. And it grew. We now run the largest focus group known to mankind, with locations in major cities all over the world. We are the first ever organization of any kind—in all of history—to contain human participants who were born into the focus group for the purpose of continuing the experiment. Participants like you."

"You...." I covered my eyes with the heels of my palms and pressed. "You made my parents give birth to me in...in an experiment?"

"Your parents signed their parental rights over to me before you were even conceived, and technically, even that was a formality. They have since been removed from the program and now live comfortably. One in Delaware, I believe. The other in Stockholm. You've never met them, but their contribution to our study is beyond compare."

"So everyone in my life knew about this but me? *Everyone knew*?"

"No. Some are informed in varying degrees at varying points in time. If it serves the program, that is."

"And it serves the program to tell me this now?"

"It does. I would even say it's crucial at this point. If you had not figured this out, Bellanueva—if you had not come to us—we may not have found you. And the results would

have been the demise of the entire program. I suppose I should thank you."

Ep 66

Shopping Therapy

"Don't you dare thank me. You...keep us in prison to sell things to people we don't know."

"It is an honor to have your life mean something."

"I don't get to choose its meaning!"

"You have chosen so many things, Bellanueva. You get as much choice as about anyone in the world gets when they are born. Your family is chosen for you. Your socioeconomic standing is predetermined. Your options for work as an adult already exist. You are free to be a strategic as you want within those parameters, though others may influence your decisions."

"You tortured Glimpses for this. For—what are you even selling?"

He shrugged. "Clothes, shoes. Cosmetics. Shampoo, shaving cream, bodywash. Things like that. And we did not *torture* Glimpses. You're off on that one."

"What are you going to call what you did to them? The 'same' as the regular world? Do people in this place get their bones scraped and their faces rearranged?"

"They do, actually, but that is beyond the point. The Glimpse is entirely my creation. Entirely. A Glimpse...it's not real, Bellanueva."

"Of course he's real. He's real. I can hold him. I can—"

"He is an assembling of ideas manifested in matter. He is a collection of parts of ideas. He does not classify as a person. And—"

"You can't go around...inventing people!"

"And there are no 'Glimpses'. There is only *one*."

I froze at that, my nose running and my eyes burning from the tears that flowed without relent. "Only...one?"

"Yes. In order to both isolate and amplify the particular expression of beauty that best serves our purposes, we gave our Glimpse

multiple aspects of self. These aspects are eliminated when they no longer serve our experiment. And amplified if they do."

"You...gave him multiple versions...of himself?"

"We did. Though we can't be clear whether he understands that they are all the same—"

"He does not! He knows and cares for each of them as if they are friends. Family. And you just...kill them off when one isn't beautiful enough? He thinks they're *real*. What the hell is wrong with you? This is *worse* than torture."

"Interesting. So he has disassociated enough from each version so entirely that he believes them to be separate entities capable of interaction."

"You don't even know what you're doing while you do it?"

"It is difficult for us to speak with the Glimpse. He does not communicate very effectively. Although some versions are more chatty than others, the information they divulge is not always useful. But the one you call 'Marrow', he *speaks* with you.

Never before have we gotten such insight into the understanding of the Glimpse. It's one of the many reasons we allowed you to go on in the focus group, Bellanueva. Though your time was almost up, you always managed to prolong it. To extend the entire experiment, really. Honestly, the version you call 'Marrow' would have been removed by now if not for you."

"You would have removed Marrow from himself?"

"We would probably have kept Helix. That expression is of much interest to the Grands."

"The—"

"The Grands are also generated for the purpose of our project. They've taken on a life of their own. Much unlike you, a human born within the group, but still, their evolution is fascinating to witness."

"You're sick. You're insane. Marrow feels *pain*. And happiness. And hope. He is a person. You can't just rip him apart and sew him together and not consider how it affects him. How it hurts him. You can't just leave him alone in a facility with no friends, no family. Just versions of himself to keep him company. You can't do that."

"We are saving lives."

"By selling things?"

"By maintaining a necessary system."

"You are a greed-filled coward."

"Call me whatever you want. But you must know that if you continue to unravel this program, you will lose the Marrow you claim to know and love."

I gasped. "You would not."

"We won't have a choice. He will dematerialize if this program ends. He will literally"—and the man held up his hands to form a ball and then let the ball fall away—"stop mattering. No more matter for Marrow."

"You can't do that."

"I can't stop it. The only way he continues to exist is if the program continues. If L.A.O.B.A.N. performs well enough to receive more funding and we keep delivering stellar results. If we keep defining beauty for our clients and they keep selling products, we get to keep Marrow."

I felt cold and hot at the same time. I knew I was close to passing out, but I was afraid to close my eyes and rest. "Why me? Why even bother? You have your Glimpse. You have your willing participants. Why me?"

"Because the participants tire of living Here or There. The Grades...they aren't permitted entrance or exit during the experiment. Some have lived in the group for years without reprieve. The only way out is removal, after which there is no reentering the program. No chance to have their names on the study. And so—"

"You thought you could give birth to Grades who don't know any better. Who don't want to leave Here or There. Who don't even know a world exists outside of the Grits and the Grands and the Glimpses. We would be complacent to work for you forever. It would be all we know. So you birthed us in the program and then tested us to see who could be smart enough to do the job."

"And you...you are smart, Bellanueva. Too smart. We feared you would discover things you shouldn't. And you did. But—"

"But in doing so I gave you information about Marrow. You watched and studied. I gave you insight you wouldn't have gotten otherwise. I get it. You already told me this."

"Not only that. You brought out of him a beauty the likes of which we've never seen. Never. You make him...indescribable."

"All this...all this for—"

"For the Glory." And Lawry smiled a bit, as if remembering a fond dream. "We thought there was a nice ring to that. Gotta love a little alliteration, I always say. All this for the Glory. For the world outside your own."

I sniffled to no avail. "You're going to send us back, aren't you?"

"Marrow must return. He needs particular care. Maintenance. And we have many, many tests to do. We must determine how this adventure has altered him. Whether he will still be usable. We will integrate a new monitoring system to keep him integrated. Health, Agility, Fitness, and Intellect Zoning system. H.A.F.I.Z. for short, though you encountered this system on the day of its demise."

I remembered Hafiz. I would never forget him dangling from the ceiling. Never forget how devastated Marrow was to learn he was gone. He had not done away with the system, but if one of his versions did...it had been Marrow all along. Losing track of the other versions of himself.

"The Glimpse can't do without it, though we've never witnessed the Glimpse destroy its own Zoning system before now. Before you." Lawry tilted his rather ordinary head as he observed me. "We have other plans for you, Bellanueva."

"Plans?"

"As you are not technically a citizen of the world, you are my intellectual property. So the plan may not be to your liking. But it will ensure that your Marrow lives on. That he is so beautiful, his funding will never cease. That the clock never hits zero. That this version of him is too valuable to terminate."

"What will you do to me?"

He thought about this and sighed. "I will let you choose. That seems best. You may

return There and continue testing and training as a Grade. We will replicate some of your findings, but they will be with new versions of Glimpses, some of which you will help me create. You will help to train new future Grades who are born Here."

"I will take the role of Cyrilus."

"Indeed. He is very dead, if you recall. We need a replacement. And that can be you."

"Or...."

"Or...one last experiment. And we keep Marrow. He matters. Possibly forever."

Ep 67

The Favorite Part

Bel was not sitting in the waiting area when I left the restroom. Instead, men in black uniforms told me I had to go with them if ever I wanted to see her again. They said if I fought, they would have to put me to sleep, and I knew that if anything like that happened, she would be gone when I opened my eyes.

So I went with them past many doors until I stood in a room much like I'd stood in many times before. There were medical beds present. Two of them.

"Hello, Marrow," a man said. He wore a dark coat and a matching set of bottoms. Pale blue eyes squinted at me. "How are you looking today?"

I did not answer the man. Strange how no words could leave my mouth, even when I wanted to demand to see Bel. Even though it was a speaking day.

"Please lie down here on this bed. The Grades will prepare your next procedure."

I did not move. Before, I would have lain down without question but now, I knew better. Now I knew there was more to life than needles and scalpels.

"I can't bring her to you until you lie down."

I sighed and made my way onto the bed. Grades came in wearing their white coats and strapped me in more tightly than ever before. I felt everything I'd been taught to feel. Like the very center of the earth was taking me back into it. Like I was the first thing ever alive. Marrow. The source of life itself.

"Very good. Here, we will bring her out to you now."

But I could not see her. I could not sit up. I only heard the jangling of the restraints on the bed next to me.

"You may say very little to him, Bellanueva," the man said. "He is more fragile than ever. And have no fear of the flash of light. It's intense but it kills any contaminants. Can't have you ill."

"Bel?" I strained against the cloths that bound me to the bed. "Bel! Leave her alone. Leave her!"

"Calm him," the man said. "He will injure himself."

"No!" I screamed. "Let her go! What are you doing to her?"

"Marrow?" I quieted in an instant. Her voice cracked when she spoke, and I could feel a mirrored tear rip through my heart. "Marrow, listen, alright?"

"Bel...why are you strapped down as well? That is not how this usually goes."

"I know. But it's alright. It's okay."

"It's not okay! It's not alright!"

"They're going to take us back."

"Bel! I don't want to go back. I want to stay here with you."

"I would love to stay with you...Marrow? Do you remember Hafiz?"

Hafiz? I thought and thought but I had never heard of it before. "No?"

"He's someone who will help sort things for you. And keep you organized and...and safe. You'll meet him soon."

"Why would I need this Hafiz person if I have you? Bel!"

Grades wheeled us through the halls and then into a room with blinding lights, so hot that they burned my eyes and skin. And when I opened my eyes once more, we were in a domed room made of glass.

Around that glass were the Grands, their feathers and scales and long necks and round eyes facing us and staring. Peering down from platforms, elevated. They did not move or speak. Only watched. What they saw, I would never know. I would never understand.

"Bel...."

"Marrow." She stopped. I realized she was crying. And the gentle sound of metal clinking meant she was trembling enough to shake her whole bed. "Tell me the best part so far."

"Bel, what is happening?"

"Please, tell me the best part so far. Please."

I could not get up. No matter how hard I wrenched my muscles. I was trapped in the bed with the Grands staring and Bel's voice growing quieter and quieter beside me. "Bel, are you alright?"

"I'm alright," she said, hushed.

"The first time we hugged. It changed my whole life. And the first time I ate."

"Tacos...."

I could not keep from crying. "Bel, please, tell them to let you go. I do not understand."

"Keep going, 'Row. Your favorite parts."

"Driving. I love when the windows are down and we hold hands."

She chuckled. "That's a top three...for me...."

"I loved what we did together when we first got to Orlando. I loved that so much."

"Top two."

"What—what's your number one?"

She convulsed, shaking the whole bed, saving her words for after her body stopped tensing. "I...like to leave that spot open. In case...."

Her voice was so far away I could not hear her. I felt my chest break open. I felt my fear swallow me. I felt the aloneness of a thousand lives lost without explanation, without me understanding what that feeling could even mean.

"Bel? Did you figure it out?"

"Mmhmm...."

"Was it...was it worth it?"

"...no."

"Please. Please don't go."

And there was a long silence. Long enough for me to forget the Grands and the Grades and the Grits. Long enough for me to forget everything but Bel.

"Marrow?"

"I'm right here."

Her breath rattled in her chest. "Will you hold my hand again?"

I tried and I tried and I screamed for them to let me out, to let me get to her.

But no one released me. I could not see her. I could barely hear her. And there was no way I could hold her hand.

"Please!" I shouted until I was sure my throat bled.

Finally, someone wheeled us closer to one another. I stretched my fingers until they almost snapped, just so I could touch my knuckles to hers.

***Cold*. Bel was cold.**

***No, please no*. "Bel?"**

"Marrow...do you think...tucking someone in...is a real thing that happens? Do people really...do that for each other?"

"I think so."

"If it is...Marrow...you tucked me in every day...since I met you. Every day."

"Let me hold her!" I called out, but no one responded. "Bel, you tuck me in every day. Every night. All the time in between. Counting up and counting down and forgetting to count at all."

But she did not hear me say it. Because her shaking stopped, and her hand went limp beside mine.

I did not think about wrinkling when I cried. I did not think about anything. There was only pain. There was only my heart dying along with hers.

And when I could no longer keep my eyes open, I heard someone say, "A new standard for beauty, then. Never seen anything quite like this. Well done. Well done, everyone."

The Grade bent as he wheeled me away from the Grands in the dome, away from Bel's body. "How are you looking today, Marrow?"

How am I...looking? Even if I had the words, even if my throat did not bleed and my blood had not gone still as the dead. Even if I had an eternity to think of a response, I could not answer. For there was only one question that mattered. And I did not know what it was. *Bel is the one who should be asking. Bel...should be....*

No matter. No matter if I matter now or not. I could not answer.

From the Mind of Teshelle Combs

Slit Throat Saga

An epic dystopian fantasy | Will Nexus Aerixon destroy the world she is trying to save? Go to amazon.com/kindle-vella and search for "Slit Throat Saga."

The Young Ones

Sociopathic kingpin rules the world | Raised—and rejected—by the most ruthless Insider alive, Charley Porter will do anything to win Everything. Go to amazon.com/kindle-vella and search for "The Young Ones."

The First Stone

An epic romance | Sanaa of Rote exists only to please her father, the King, by marrying the High Prince of an allied realm. And she will succeed. She must. If she can bear to swallow her hatred for the man to whom she must yield every fragment of her power. Go to amazon.com/kindle-vella and search for "The First Stone."

The First Nymph

A haunting romance | High Prince Maxos will stop at nothing to force a marriage out of Queen Eilyn for the good fortune of his own realm. Eilyn will have to destroy the Prince along with his ambitions to protect the women of Orega...if she can manage to keep her hands off him. Go to amazon.com/kindle-vella and search for "The First Nymph."

The First Dryad

An enchanted romance | Aia spent her life in hiding...until her secret was discovered and she was taken to the Palace in chains. Now, among the last crop of an ancient arboreal race, she will have to prove herself useful to the High Prince to survive. But alas, love is ruin. And the last of one race might become the first in another. Go to amazon.com/kindle-vella and search for "The First Dryad."

The Underglow

A vampire love story | Meet Aurelie and Alexander. But be careful...he bites. Go to amazon.com/kindle-vella and search for "The Underglow."

Books

Kindle and Paperback

Slit Throat Saga

"My people," he said, yelling over the toning, "let's celebrate. For today, the one who breaks the laws of nature, the one who moves the unmovable, the one who tests the very hands of God, will be set back on the right path. The Fight is not in vain."

He turned with a flourish to watch with us all as a translucent synthetix blade, held tight in the Moral's fist, sliced across the throat of the girl. A gurgle, then her blonde head flopped forward. Her blood gushed brilliant red. One would think it meant that the Fight was mistaken, that she was just like everyone else—a normal human with no unearthly capabilities, no deadly tendencies. Her blood seemed pure and red, filled with iron just like it should be. But after a few seconds, as her strength faded, the red diluted and her blood ran clear as a mountain river.

She was Meta. Just like they thought and I'm sure as they determined when she was confined in the House of Certainty for questioning. No true metal in her veins. No metal in her whole body. Not even metal in her mind. Instead she could pull it to her. She was a magnet. An abomination. And if left uncaught and unkilled, her kind would destroy the world.

The people—my people—cheered along with the Best Of Us as the Meta's watery blood poured over her small breasts, down her loose linen shirt, over the wooden platform, and through the street. It always amazed me how long Meta could bleed, how much life they held in their bodies. We all waited until the flow pooled beneath our feet, Ender Stream blessing us with one final reminder: *If you are us, you live, and if you are them, you die.*

"Well, Nex," Onur said with a little sigh as the crowd began to disperse, shoes squelching in the remains of the Meta girl, "what must be done is done." He brushed my thick, silver curls behind my ear so he could kiss my temple again, his favorite habit. His pale skin seemed to shine against my dusty red complexion. He looked tired, but he smiled. "We should get something to eat, yes?"

I smiled back at him, turning and tiptoeing so I could reach his lips with my own. His were soft and yielding, warm and inviting. Mine were not quite as full, not quite as tender. I met his eyes, ensuring that my gaze said exactly what I needed it to. *All Fight, no fear.* "Yes, let's eat. We can say cheers to the next one to be found."

I stepped through the Stream, one hand tight in my love's. The other hand I kept stuffed in the pocket of my cotton dress, clenched, but not so firmly that my fingernails might draw blood from my palm. That would not do. For the Stream soaking through my shoes was no less damned than the blood coursing through my veins.

Careful, Nex.

Careful.

Books

Kindle and Paperback

The Underglow

I confessed to myself that I had paid very little attention to the countless governesses who attempted to explain the general rules of romantic engagement for Femmes of my stature and upbringing. But despite my lack of knowledge of general rules, I had a general sense that I was breaking them, whatever they were. Generally speaking, of course.

Closer should have made me nervous. I was not nervous, however, and so closer I went until there was no separation between his hips and mine. This was a relief to me—one difficult to explain. For I did not think there could ever be such closeness between another living thing and myself. Truly, I did not think, though they claimed to desire it, that any other living thing wanted to be so close to me.

<<You withhold>>, Alexander meant to me, pulling my bottom lip between his before pressing his mouth fully to mine. I felt only the slightest prick of his fangs, for he had not lengthened them. With my head nearly swimming, I wondered if he would sink those fangs into me as he once did. But no. Instead, he intended. <<I will be patient>>.

I detested patience. It was a monster that society told its victims was required, but really, it only convinced us all to work longer hours while they fattened us up for the slaughter. What is the point of patience? Who does it serve but the impatient ones?

I wrapped my arms around his waist and held firmly, but he released my grip rather easily.

<<Patience>>. With a last touch of his thumb to my lip and a final probe of his considerate eyes, he stepped away. <<I will find who hurt you>>.

I truthfully thought he had forgotten about this, as it had left my mind entirely. The idea that he would seek some vengeance on my behalf made my hands go numb, for it led me to envision Alexander strung up in a dark dungeon, awaiting Sleep. Surely he would be captured. Surely he would be enslaved once more. Surely I would not be able to save him. Chivalry was not something I required from this pyre.

But he looked at me—some small distance between us—in such a way that I could not believe it was chivalry compelling him.

<<You do not wish me to find them>>, he meant. The feeling of his meaning came slow and hot, like waves against a stone on too warm of a day. Or like standing too close to a flame. This is what it felt like for Alexander to be cross with me.

I wondered if I should be worried that I enjoyed the feeling.

And then I felt a shift in him, or rather, felt it come from him. <<I will go>>.

Books

Kindle and Paperback

The First Dryad

"You dropped your book," the Second Prince said with a smirk. "Did you do that on purpose, Little Tree?" He folded his ink-stained hands together in front of him, his elbows on the desk.

I bent and snatched the book up, clutching it to my chest. "Why would I drop a book on purpose?"

He tilted his head. "To appear helpless."

"Why would I put so much effort into feigning a state to which I have already fallen victim?"

His eyebrows raised, his stormy eyes lightening for a moment. "You are a victim to helplessness?"

"Well, I am here in this Palace against my will. And I cannot help myself except to accelerate my own demise if I so chose, which I do not. So yes, I would say I am quite helpless. And so, if I drop a book, it is not some strategy. I am merely nervous. And now you have made fun of me for it."

"Hmm...." He picked up his quill after studying me for just a bit and made as if he would write again. But before he touched it to his paper, he looked back up at me, surprised that I still stood before him. "Will you not...*go*, then, since I have made you so nervous?"

I knew how ferociously I blushed, and how my heart squeezed almost to the point beyond beating in my chest, and how my hands gripped the book too tightly. But I could not, for any reason or after any amount of urging myself, convince my feet to move.

The Second Prince laughed, but not the happy sort, and stood up from his seat. He approached me, his white shirt unbuttoned at the top and his brown breeches nicely cut and perfectly hemmed. When he was very close to me, he reached out to take the book from my hands.

I let him do this, of course, because he was a Monarch of the Realm, and who was I to deny him? Except when I looked down at my arms, the book was still pressed against my bosom, and his hand had retreated, for I had dodged its advance with the slightest deflection.

He was very surprised then, as was I, and his dark-blue eyes glittered with amusement. "May I see your book please, Honorable Tree?"

I bit my lip as I handed it to him. And then, because I did not know what to do with my empty hands, I clenched the formerly smooth fabric along the sides of my sage green dress.

The Prince traced his fingers across the leather cover of the book, and I felt my chest burn. I gasped at this response, for it was not allowable for me to think about his fingers or the way they moved so lightly over the brown leather. I was not meant to wonder what those same hands would feel like wandering over my skin.

His eyes flicked up at me when I gasped, but then, when he saw I had nothing to say, he continued with his examination of the book.

Books

Kindle and Paperback

Core Series

Ava is the kind of girl who knows what's real and what isn't. Nothing in life is fair. Nothing is given freely. Nothing is painless. Every foster kid can attest to those truths, and Ava lives them every day. But when she meets a family of dragon shifters and is chosen to join them as a rider, her very notion of reality is shaken. She doesn't believe she can let her guard down. She doesn't think she can let them in—especially not the reckless, kind-eyed Cale. To say yes to him means he would be hers—her dragon and her companion—for life. But what if Ava has no life left to give?

The System Series

1 + 1 = Dead. That's the only math that adds up when you're in the System. Everywhere Nick turns, he's surrounded by the inevitability of his own demise at the hands of the people who stole his life from him. That is, until those hands deliver the bleeding, feisty, eye-rolling Nessa Parker. Tasked with keeping his new partner alive, Nick must face all the ways he's died and all the things he's forgotten.

Nessa might as well give up. The moment she gets into that car, the moment she lays her hazel eyes on her new partner, her end begins. It doesn't matter that Nick Masters can slip through time by computing mathematical algorithms in his mind. It doesn't matter how dark and handsome and irresistibly cold he is. Nessa has to defeat her own shadows. Together and alone, Nick and Nessa make sense of their senseless fates and fight for the courage to change it all. Even if it means the System wins and they end up...

well...dead.

Poetry

Thoughts Like Words

Let There Be Nine Series

- *Let There Be Nine Vol 1*: **Enneagram Poetry**
- *Let There Be Nine Vol 2*: **Enneagram Poetry**

For Series: Words laced together on behalf of an idea, a place, a world.

- **For Her**
- **For Him**
- **For Them**
- **For Us**

Love Bad Series: Poems About Love. Not Love Poems.

- **Love Bad**
- **Love Bad More**
- **Love Bad Best**

Standalone Poetry Books:

BREATH LIKE GLASS

Poems for love that never lasts.

Girl Poet

A collection of poems on the passion, privilege, and pain of being (or not quite being) a girl.

FRAMELESS

A collection of poems for the colors that make life vibrant, from their perspective, so we may share in what they might think and feel.

This One Has Pockets

Narrative poetry about a girl who is near giving up and the boy who tries to save her.

ON THE NATURE OF HINGES

A series of poetic questions from the perspective of someone who has been left behind more than once.

Gray Child

A unique expression of being more than one race, written by a Caribbean American woman, for anyone who cares to read.

Contact Teshelle Combs

Instagram | @TeshelleCombs

Facebook | Vella World Of Teshelle Combs

Leave A Review

A good review is how you breathe life into my story. Please leave *Tuck Me In* an Amazon review and tell a friend how much you love this story.

Made in the USA
Middletown, DE
06 June 2023

32177009R00203